67,000 words

The Grand Adventures

of Jeff and Dan:

The Dragon War

by

Eric Keith Middleton

D1528431

Contents

To Stacy and Elijah.

Dramatis Personae

<u>Dragon Slayer</u>

Danvel (He slays Dragons!)

<u>Sleipnir</u>

Jeff (He helps slay Dragons!)

<u>Patron Dragons</u>

Leviathan (Patron Dragon of Water)

Fafnir (Patron Dragon of Fire)

James (Patron Dragon of Earth)

Tiamat (Patron Dragon of Wind)

<u>Dragons</u>

Hourig (Fire Dragon. He's old)

Aturdokht (Fire Dragon. He's not)

Lynnaedra (Water Dragon)

<u>Humanoid</u>

Gunther (He's kind of a klutz)

Gale (Barmaid. She's also hot)

Murlan (He's a wizard. Not a great one)

Non-humanoid

Bernard (Behemoth)

Benedict (Behemoth)

Introduction

Excerpt from Benedict the Great Historian's *History of the World*

The Great Dragon Age was ended due to a war and not the war that most people thought. Dragonia and Wyrmvale had been in an on and off war for a few centuries. Battles were few and far in between, but when they did happen it usually ended up being bloody.

Leviathan was the Patron Dragon of Dragonia at the time. She fully endorsed the war and was frequently seen giving the troops pointers on warfare and strategies (Some thought this breached the rules of the Dragon Law which clearly states that Dragons shall have no involvement in the wars between men). Having been alive most of the war had given her some unique insights. The war had been rough for Dragonia, causing shortages of nearly everything. Armor and food were becoming scarce even though Leviathan tried to downplay it to everyone.

The reason for the shortage was indeed who they were at war with. Wyrmvale was the crop center for the whole continent of Draco. Their fertile land let even the most difficult crops grow nearly the whole year. Highly trained Gnomes brought the land to life in ways that most people never thought possible. In addition to the foodstuffs that Wyrmvale provided, it also housed the biggest populace of Dwarves in the world. Dwarves were the premier artists of armory and weaponry. They created perhaps the most intricately beautiful and utile armor ever seen to humanoid and other miscellaneous races.

James was the Patron Dragon of Wyrmvale and was said to be the fairest Dragon of all time. As such, he never supported the war since the beginning of his term as Patron Dragon. While relatively young as Patron Dragons go, he led the Wyrms with wisdom and grace beyond his years.

Dragonia lay in the west, Wyrmvale in the south. In the east stood Salamandra. Choosing to remain neutral in the war, Salamandra shared whatever supplies they could with both nations. Fafnir, their Patron Dragon, was a wise old Dragon and disliked most senseless conflict. Salamandra was the only other country with a port and used it to ship its many ores to Dragonia. The country was full of several active volcanoes and left only one safe place for one city, Hellbender. Despite its name, the city was a marvel.

In north was Drakeland. A place of mystery, death, and snow. Tiamat, their Patron Dragon, hadn't been seen in nearly a century and no one knew much about the north at the time. Rumors held that the Yeti did magic rituals that kept people from traveling too far north and interacting with them.

Little did they all know that in less than a year, all of their lives were about to change dramatically. A war was coming. A war the likes that no one has ever seen before.

Prologue

You might not think by looking at me but I'm one of the mightiest dragon slayers in the realm... Well I was before this happened to me. What do I mean by this? I used to be 6 foot tall and the width of a door. Now? I'm 3 feet tall and the width of a doggy door (not to say that dire wolves don't grow to be large). Even my great steed Jeff the Sleipnir just looks like an 8 legged pony. I was once Danvel the Dragon Slayer but now... I don't know who I am, but I will return to my former self. I swear it.

Chapter 1 - Self Discovery

Dragonia

Knight training ground

Sunrise

The sun had just begun draping itself over the land unmasking the heavily used training grounds in front of me. The sun also unmasked the thirteen trainees marching in line to the instructor.

Their armor shone cerulean, a distinct cerulean similar to that of Leviathan herself. Despite the armor having new faces and bodies, you could tell it had been used before by the battle scars adorning them. Leviathan was Dragonia's Patron Dragon and considered mother to all the Water Dragons. She controlled the oceans of the world, and gave life to the rivers, lakes, and current, thus making the country the principal procurers of fish and rare goods on the continent. She was also the only Patron Dragon I had come into contact with. Fair and just (for a Dragon), she treated the people of her country well, at least in my opinion.

My armor stood stark black with piping of white in contrast to the trainees; the colors of Dragon Slayers. I had received it on a stint in Asgard fighting Frost Giants with Thor and Odin. After I helped the Asgardians finish their war, Jeff, the Sleipnir sleeping beside me, was given to me and Sindri and Brokkr forged our armor. It was a glorious time of war and mirth, and gave way to the great friendship I now have with Jeff (perhaps the greatest friendship of all time... or something).

We are at war with the realm of Wyrmvale." The Dragonian training knight barked at the trainees. I had snuck into the training camp to test the limits of my new... shape. Sneaking because I wasn't quite ready to announce that I had been shrunk to look like a child. Jeff was just as eager to see what we could do, or he would be if he wasn't sleeping. " So today we will be facing the obstacle course, the Crusher. Don't be fooled by its name, it will eviscerate you too. What it will also do, is train you in the rigors of war. A knight must be ready at all times; despite what they have gone through, to fight at a moment's notice," he barked again towards the recruits. The Knight stood taller than any of them. The parts of his body without the cerulean armor showed the many scars of war.

"Excuse me, sir. When will we be learning to face against... D... D.... Dragons?" a particularly frail knight trainee asked. His face looked young compared to the rest of the recruits and his eyes held the light of youth and hope in them. Not the man for a war. Not the man I'd want to see change into a soldier...a killer.

Hopefully you never have to experience it, son," the instructor replied. "Dragons are forbidden to fight in the wars of humans. Dragon law forbids even the slightest involvement. The only time you would ever face a Dragon, God forbid it ever happens, is when that Dragon suffers from the Arcane Rot. The Dragon is driven insane by the very magics that bind it to this realm. A Water Dragon out to sea for too long or an Earthwyrm who has spent too much time hoarding its treasures underground... but we haven't had to worry about that much anymore since Danvel came around." That's me! He's talking about me! Well me… before this. Stupid short legs.

I had slain more dragons than anyone else. Mostly because I was the only Dragon Slayer left. Dragons that had suffered from the Arcane Rot or that had simply breached the Dragon law and attacked Humanoids. They became perverse versions of themselves and whatever goodness that was supposedly in them was washed away.

Recruits, line up and face the Eviscerator," the knight said with a smile. He stamped his feet and they all lined up.

But I thought it was called the Crusher," the same recruit from before said, nervously. There wasn't a gulping that i saw, but i definitely think i heard one.. He peeked his head from the line and awkwardly gawked at the instructor.

"Don't worry, it'll do that too," the instructor said with a devilish grin. The thirteen recruits, Jeff (sleepwalking… he does that), and I made our way over to the Crusher/ Eviscerator. The training device was divided into six different parts, each meant to represent the potential situations a knight might face.

The first part consisted of the climb; a series of swinging ropes that you had to climb and switch between to reach the top of it. To this day, I had no idea what situation I would use this in, but the knights insisted on it.

The second part, my favorite part, was the drop. Recruits had to work themselves through a maze of wood and wire to find their way out, all the while avoiding the dreaded drops into the moat below. It took skill and a little bit of misdirection to get out first, but if you understood the secrets, you could make it out faster than it takes a Frost Giant to get beaten.

The third part was the descent. This was conceivably the hardest part as a person would have to guide themselves down the path full of waters that were rushing at different speeds and directions without falling over. Any who fell over were rushed down into the moat (the water speeds were provided by the on-site Water Dragon).

The second half of the Eviscerator/Crusher was meant to be completely different. After swimming out of the moat or successfully working your way through the descent, you had to face the instructors in a basic sword training exercise.

After that, the on-site Water Dragon directed a team exercise on fighting dragons. Despite the fact that Dragons didn't fight in the wars, that didn't mean that random Dragons suffering from Arcane Rot or who didn't agree with Dragon laws wouldn't attack the troops.

The last part was an ambush from hidden training officers. They hid behind camouflaged barriers and charged the unit as a team. After all the men had gone through, they still had to keep their wits about them.

While a man might be able to go through this course easily, it was made much harder by the fact that they had armor on. It was to help simulate the hardships of life as a knight. After marching through unknown and unpredictable conditions, a knight must be ready to face whatever comes at them.

As a Dragon Slayer, I had the instincts to easily navigate the course... when I was normal size, at least. While most of the recruits had made their way through the maze, I was still stuck on the climb. Despite having the same strength I used to have, my arm reach wasn't what I was accustomed to. I had reached the last rope but couldn't quite swing it to the ledge of the maze. As I continued to try and swing over to the ledge, the meek recruit from before came over. "Need a hand?" he asked as he watched me swing back and forth.

"You think? I seem to have a bit of a problem. My arms are so short," I said with a proud but begging voice. He reached his hand up and pulled me over. As I reached the stable floor, I started to take the recruit in. He rose to about five feet and a half. A small size for a future knight but given my current stature, I found it slightly off putting.

"Aren't you a little young for this," he asked unassumingly. My rage rose up but I quieted it down quickly. This young boy had no idea what had befallen me and I shouldn't take it out on him. Or at least I shouldn't yet. Revenge is always better later.

"Actually, I'm older than you," I said with a smile. "My name's Danvel." I put out my hand for an introductory handshake.

The young recruit replied by giving out what could only be referred to as a guffaw and ignoring my hand. "You can't be Danvel. I can't see a famous Dragon Slayer only being three foot tall." I kept my hand extended but he didn't go for it. He must have been smarter than I thought because if he took it this time, I was going to crush his hand.

"I'll explain it to you later tonight when you buy me some mead for helping you get through the rest of the training course. Now let's move, whatever your name is," I said as I dashed forward into the maze. The maze had five entrances. While most recruits avoided the center, I knew the tricks of the course. At least I hoped I did. Sometimes instructors change things and I don't like those instructors.

"Gunther," he replied. What an awful name. "How do you know where to go?" he asked as he followed behind me. Being about twice my height, he easily kept up with me.

"The maze is less about finding your way out and more about being sure of where you're going. A knight must be sure of his actions and not hesitate when heading into battle," I said while darting around a corner. "The floor paneling of the maze can read how long you stay in one spot. If you hesitate for too long the flooring will drop out. Mage trickery!"

We continued running and soon reached the end. Only two recruits (other than Gunther) had made it through and were working their way down the rapids. The one recruit was being pushed towards the edge in the current, but the one in the lead actually seemed like he was in control.

"What's the trick to this one, then?" Gunther asked as he almost ran past me into the water.

"LUCK," I yelled as I jumped in. Gunther tumbled down behind me, caught between two different currents. I was successfully maintaining a one current path, but my smaller frame didn't afford me much help. I was trying to touch the bottom with my legs but was mostly just flailing them around helplessly.

"I ....gurgle gargle.... hate waterrrrr," Gunther yelled behind me. His descent had stopped thanks to a whirlpool and he was slowly drifting towards the drop off to the moat.

After a moment or two, I had reached ground level and escaped the current of the waters. The lead recruit had made it the whole way and was already starting his sword practice with the instructor. I looked back to see Gunther in the moat, Dragon paddling his way towards me. The other recruits had already begun lining up waiting for the instructors to turn their eye on them.

I walked to the edge of the moat and extended a hand. "Need a hand?"

"If you wouldn't mind terribly. I seem to have a bit of a problem," Gunther said with a smile.

I pulled him up one handedly and placed him upon dry land. "Well you made it through the truly hard part of the training exercise. Let's hope your sword play is better than your ability to wade through water." As we walked backed to where they were doing the sword instruction, the instructor barreled out from between the recruits in a furor.

"Who the hell let a damn child onto my training course!" he yelled as he charged towards us. Gunther put himself between us to try and explain, but the knight plowed him over. By the time he reached me, Jeff had already galloped to my side and my face was beet red with anger. Behind him followed the instructors, recruits, and the Water Dragon. That was when he made the mistake at pointing his finger at me.

"What the hell do you think you're doing, kid! You could get yourself......," his inability to finish his sentence came from the excruciating pain his hand. Despite being armored, my Dragon

Slayer strength had crushed it. Upon seeing the agony he was in, the Water Dragon charged at me. That's where Jeff came in.

"NEIGHHHH," Jeff said as he struck the Water Dragon with six of his legs. The Water Dragon staggered out of its charge and into the moat. Jeff spun around in a circle and put on his fiercest face for the recruits (not that a pony sized Sleipnir was fierce looking). I marched back to the knight and put my finger his face.

"What I am doing is exercising my right as a Dragon Slayer to participate in the training of recruits. Don't you know who I am? I am Danvel the Great Dragon Slayer," I said with great pride. To my dismay, the instructors and recruits all laughed at me. To their dismay (and with Jeff's help) they all ended up in the moat.

I picked Gunther off the ground and stood him up straight. "You okay, kid?" I asked with true sincerity. He tried to stand up straight but it took him a few seconds.

"I think so, Mr. Danvel," he said as he looked around at the suddenly empty training grounds. "Where did everyone go?"

I smiled as I replied, "They went for a dip."

We left the training grounds in a mild hurry, hoping that the castle guards would be too busy helping the instructors and recruits out of the water. We found ourselves back into town by noon. "So what part of Dragonia do you hail from, Gunther?" I asked as we entered the market, Jeff in tow.

The market was bustling with all kinds of townsfolk and Dragons. Mixed amongst the citizens of Dragonia was the occasional band of Elves, a small horde of Goblins, and a pride of Lionmen. Jeff liberated a few apples from a nearby cart while the cart-owner's attention was elsewhere and shared them.

"Couldn't give you a straight answer, Mr. Danvel. A Dragon attacked my home when I was young and killed my family. At least that's what I was told. I was only a baby. The Dragon destroyed most of the village. When all was said and done there was a dead Water Dragon at the scene, presumably defending the village and an Earthwyrm was seen wandering off. It's why I decided to become a knight and help fight against those nasty Earthwyrms and the people who support them."

I didn't reply for a little bit as we passed through the market and bought some small supplies for the day. "My family was killed by Dragons, too. It's one of the reasons I became a Dragon Slayer. That and it's in my bloodline. Word was that an old Dragon had gotten the Arcane Rot and tore through the countryside." We stayed quiet for a few minutes, mulling the exchange of information we just had.

"Sometimes I wish that the Dragons didn't exist, when I think about my parents. I'd never have grown up too fast. Wouldn't have had to be the only Dragon Slayer left alive, let alone the smallest in history. I mean what am I? Am I a Dragon Slayer still? Most people seem to just want laugh at me."

Gunther replied with the same silence that I had just given him. "I think despite all the Dragons have done that you have to recognize the importance they have in the balance of life. See, we Humanoids are mostly of the physical nature. Sure there are some that are more magical than others; elves, fairies, etc. Dragons are half physical and half magical. They protect the lands from the beings of pure magic that we can't face. The Patron Dragons also help keep the world in balance," he said after a while.

I gave a half smile. "I see you've done your research on the matter." We walked through to the other side of the market and sat down beside the main fountain of the town square. Axdremaria, the capital and main port of Dragonia, was full of wonders that many had travelled across sea and continent to see.

Fountains and water works adorned the streets and passageways. The Castle of Leviathan was actually built atop the sea to prevent anyone from storming it. All of this was done with the power of Leviathan herself. While Dragonians took this for granted and foreigners travelled to see it, I felt that it was too much power for one creature to hold.

"After I was orphaned by the Dragon, I grew up in a monastery and spent a lot of time in the library. I had spent a lot of time trying to track down my lineage, but my parents had just moved here and no one had really known them. So, I guess I don't really know who I'm supposed to be either, Mr. Danvel."

A gave a soft chuckle, "Two adventurers on a quest of discovery, then?"

"NEIGH!!," Jeff replied as he finished his last apple. His eyes narrowed and he gave me a look that I knew too well. He hated being left out.

"Three adventurers, I mean," I said in between laughs.

Chapter 2 - The Bards at the Bar

Dragonia

The Leviathan Pub

Evening

The Leviathan Pub was the biggest pub in Dragonia. It also had just received an award from me for the least original name for a pub. Serving Humanoids and Dragons required a massive building.

So massive, it actually rivaled the size of the Leviathan Castle. It was a place for socialization, information, and for barriers to be torn down between species. Besides the information part, I hated it.

"Mr. Danvel, this is the greatest place ever," Gunther exclaimed with an excitement that I assume only living in a monastery could create. Gunther had just sat down with several mead glasses (at my request) and stared at me patiently. I only took notice after the first gulp of mead was down my gullet.

"Yes, you want something?" I asked smacking my lips at the well-made mead. Jeff had begun drinking some of the mead as well much to Gunther's dismay. Apparently he had never seen a Sleipnir drink from a mead glass. It was, as I would describe it, glorious.

"I believe that you promised me earlier that you would tell me how you came to be this size. Unless, the great Danvel the Dragon Slayer is also a liar," Gunther said as he sipped at his mead. He made a sour face and I guessed it was probably the first time he had mead.

"You could be a politician with a forked tongue like that," I said with a slight chuckle. "Well, where to begin...," and that was when she walked in. Gale, the Leviathan Pub's best... well everything. Men have escaped a siren's song just to see her beauty. I was on my way to Axdremaria to court her properly when this befell me. We had been an on and off couple for years but I was ready to become more. Gunther noticed my eyes following her.

"Who the heck is that?" he asked, oblivious as he always seemed to be. I slapped the boy upside the head.

"How long have you lived in Dragonia and haven't heard of Gale the Vixen? Men have swum all the way from Asgard to witness her beauty. Comparable to Aphrodite herself!" Gunther looked dumbfounded. "I can't let her see me like this, Gunther."

"Do you think she'll recognize you in your short stature," He asked looking slightly baffled at the whole situation.

I looked him dead in the eye and said, "no one ever forgets this beard." Right on cue, Gale looked over at us and smiled. It was a devilish smile. The kind of smile that made you wish it was you that she was smiling at and not the situation that you were in. The kind of smile that everyone in the room turned around to notice.

"Danvellll, oh Danvellll. Is that you? Of course that's you, No one ever forgets that beard," She called from across the room. Her voice had a tinge of sweetness in it but an overwhelming amount of bitterness. I loved it. Then the whispers began between tables. It was also when the other two glasses of mead became empty and my stomach became more full (I drank them very fast). She slinked over to the table and leaned over towards me. "I remember you being a bit taller... and perhaps a wee bit wider. You look like a child now."

"I still work just like a man," I yelled, perhaps a little too loud. I looked around as more people started to look at us. I turned and pointed at all of them. "And anyone here who doubts that I'm still the Dragon Slayer I used to be can face me themselves!"

"Now, now, Danvel. Maybe when you're all grown up again you can come around for some more fun," she said with a wink. Laughter came in an uproar from nearly the whole bar. I responded by launching myself to the nearest table full of knights and starting an epic bar fight. A left hook here and a right jab there sent most of the men unconscious and the others running for the door.

"Who else wants some!" I yelled as I crawled atop their table. Jeff stood behind me, drinking the mead out of the glasses of the disposed knights. Gunther had begun to stand but thought better of it and hid under the table. Other challengers rushed to the table and I met them all eagerly. Soon we had disposed of most of the Humanoid contenders when the Dragons started to take interest.

"Hark, Danvel. If you be the Dragon Slayer of tales, then show us your wits in battle. A true test. Follow us to the arena, young one," a Water Dragon and her troupe challenged. We agreed and followed the Dragons to the arena on the outskirts of town. The Fire Dragons lit the beacons as all the others took their places on the one side of the arena. In times of peace, the arena would hold events where representatives, Humanoid or Dagon, would come from each country, and sometimes different continents, to participate. Now it sat idle.

"Are you sure you want to do this?" Gunther asked nervously. Jeff let out a long burp beside him in reply. Gunther looked almost ready to pass out from the smell.

"I agree with Jeff," I replied. "Besides, these Dragons are as drunk as I am. Plus, I have you and Jeff at my side. Worst case scenario is you accidentally get killed!" Gunther gulped before replying.

"Me? But I don't know the first thing about fighting Dragons, Mr. Danvel. I don't want to die," Gunther said with obvious fear in his voice.

"Don't be too scared. This is just a friendly brawl between a Dragon Slayer, his horse, his knight buddy, and three Dragons," I said with a smile.

"But, I'm not a knight," Gunther said frantically. I ignored him and turned towards the Dragons.

The Water Dragon, obviously the leader, or whatever, of the trio stepped forward. She was bigger than the average Water Dragon, which usually meant much older. She had blue hair that looked similar to a flowing river. She was obviously a powerful Dragon. "My name is Lynnaedra," she started, "and these are my two companions, Hourig, and his son, Aturdokht. We expect this to be a fair brawl. No swords, no claws. Just our wits and strength."

"You know who I am," I replied, "this is my loyal steed, Jeff, and my …well... this is Gunther. We agree to terms," I said with a smile. "Give me and my team a minute to get ready." We walked back towards our side of the arena and I pulled my sword off. The sword stood a good six feet tall and as wide as a Dragon's leg. It was the only thing I had on me at the time of my miniaturization that hadn't shrunk with me. It had become a pain to carry, but I was getting used to it.

"That's a mighty big sword for someone your size," Gunther commented as he made sure his armor was tight. Not that it mattered. If a Dragon wanted, he could have made short work of Gunther's armor. They gave all the recruits the bad armor.

"It didn't used to be so big to me," I replied as I took off Jeff's spiked armor and made sure he was ready.

"Why carry it then? Seems like a mighty big burden." Gunther didn't seem to know when it was a good time to stop.

"It was my father's," I said plainly. "Dragedreper is its name." I lifted it into the air so Gunther could marvel at its beauty. It stood stark black, matching my armor, and never needed to be sharpened. "We all have our burdens to carry, anyways. Now let's get a move on. Try and avoid their hits for now, Gunther. You might not be our best fighter at the moment, but you can serve as a good distraction. Jeff, you know what to do." I nodded my head at Jeff and he got a nasty smile on his face.

We reached the center of the ring where the Dragons were waiting. "Ready?" Lynnaedra asked impatiently. It was unusual for Dragons to be impatient but these three didn't seem to be your usual Dragons.

"As we'll ever be," Gunther mumbled under his breath. Lynnaedra let out a roar and the battle was met. When her battle cry ended, I launched myself full force at her, knocking her and I back towards the end of the arena. As we came out of the roll I induced, I jumped off her, turned around and laid two haymakers to her torso.

"By Leviathan's might, you must be Danvel. I have never been struck so hard in my life," She said as she recoiled from my strikes. I looked back at the center of the arena where Gunther was running hopelessly from Hourig and Jeff was giving Aturdokht a run for his money. Damn, that horse could fight when he was drunk off his rocker.

"You should feel my punches when I'm sober then," I said as I charged towards her. She was ready for me though and gave me a clean strike with her tail, causing me to stumble and roll backwards. That only made me angry. I jumped at her tail and grabbed it, encasing it with my arms. If I had my larger frame, I could have thrown the dragon. At the present, I was just trying to hold on for dear life.

"What are you doing?" Lynnaedra asked with alarm in her voice. Apparently she thought I had some unseen strategy as she flailed her tail about and down at the ground. I began to climb up her tail and towards her hair. Sure enough, her hair felt as much water as it looked. I almost slipped off, but dug my heels in hard. Once I was stabilized, I worked my way through her … river hair and to her head. Then I let loose. She retaliated by rolling over on top of me. I held on as best I could as she flattened me again and again. Eventually I got some leverage and lifted her clean off the ground, and body slammed her. I followed up with an elbow drop and a few punches.

She backed off and waved her defeat. "I shall have two headaches tomorrow, Danvel. One from the mead and the other from your fists." We both had a good laugh at her statement and walked back to the other contenders. Jeff and Aturdokht were still fighting it out while Hourig had Gunther pinned down with his tail. Gunther kept struggling but it looked like Hourig had taken to sleeping.

"A draw," I declared to them. "I believe this calls for a celebration. Back to the pub!" Everyone cheered in agreeance. Gunther stayed flat on the ground as the rest of us started to walk away. Eventually he decided he would stop pouting and caught up with us.

We all made our way back and found seats together. Maybe it was the mead talking, but these Dragons didn't seem as bad as the others I've encountered. "So what brings you three together?" I asked as I signaled mead for our party. Luckily Gale wasn't there at the moment to mock me anymore.

"We could ask you the same thing, Danvel. We were adventuring Dragons who traveled around the world separately and we figured we'd do it again, but this time with some company. The world has such glorious sights. It would be a shame not to share them with a good friend." She pounded back some of her mead and patted her teammates on the back. "Well, enough about our trio, what brings your group together," Lynnaedra asked with keen interest. We were sort of an odd group. A midget, a pony with a drinking problem, and a knight wannabe.

"Well I just picked up this runt earlier today," I replied pointing and chuckling at Gunther. "And this fine beast," I said as I motioned to the passed out drunk Jeff, "is my best friend, Jeff. Given to me by the Asgardians. As far as what we're doing. A quest of self-discovery. Hell if I know where that leads us though."

"Quests of self-discovery often lead us where we least expect," Hourig spoke. His voice sounded as gravely as he looked. You could tell he was an old Dragon as his skin didn't glow with the same light as most Fire Dragons did. Aturdokht on the other hand was glowing quite brightly.

"Speaking of where this adventure leads us. I think maybe we should get a destination first," Gunther said, perhaps a bit nervously. Young ones were always nervous about adventure. He took a bigger than average gulp from his mead glass as he looked at me. "And you owe me a story." He apparently didn't have the courage to bring it up again without the mead.

"I suppose I do. So have any of you ever heard of an Acid Dragon," I asked as I took a swig of mead. Everyone shook their head negatively. "It's a rare type of Dragon magic problem. While some Dragons will suffer from Arcane Rot, others will be mutated into something extremely dangerous. A Water Dragon can become Geyser Dragon and can't control its own water powers. A Fire Dragon becomes a Volcano Dragon. Essentially, it takes a Dragon's power and makes it volatile. An Acid Dragon is what becomes of a Mud Dragon. Vicious and can lay waste to villages in minutes. So I went to the magician Murlan to provide me with some magical protection."

Lynnaedra looked in awe. "You know the great Merlin? We were hoping to finally meet him on this adventure of ours." She sat up in her seat more attentively.

"And right there is the mistake that I made, Lynnaedra." I took another long swig and finished my glass. "This wasn't Merlin, the greatest wizard of the world. This was Murlan, someone who apparently didn't know what they were doing. So he casts the protection spell and I go off to fight the Dragon, unbeknownst to me that I am half my normal size." I gestured to my current state of being.

"So how did you stop the Dragon?" Gunther asked with keen interest. The three Dragons and several others in the bar were also listening intently. One man nearly fell of his seat in anticipation or because he was way too drunk.

"He uhhh he died of laughter….," I answered as I swiped Gunther's glass and finished his mead, too.

"This is surely a joke, "Hourig said standing with a bit of impatience. He apparently didn't like to think that I was leading them on a wild goose sprite chase.

"He was laughing so hard when I told him to stop his rampage that he accidentally swallowed the acid falling off his body and he melted from the inside out. Apparently the magic that altered him did not alter his innards." The bar reacted with some stunned silence and a bit of stifled laughter; the patrons didn't want a repeat of earlier. "That is when I found out I was not the man I used to be. If Jeff hadn't been sleeping at the time I'm sure we would've noticed." Jeff smacked his lips in recognition that his name had been said and went back to sleep.

Lynnaedra stood up and proudly proclaimed, "And brought us the man in front of us today; Dragon Slayer and bar fight specialist! Here, here!" Everyone in the bar repeated the cheers and drank up. We ordered another round and sat back down.

"So you've beaten up Humanoids and Dragons, Danvel; what's next for your adventure in self-discovery? Answer Gunther's question," Hourig commanded as he took a massive drink. He drank more than I had seen any Dragon drink before and seemed barely affected.

"I was thinking about heading to the Dragon Slayer Temple. Old Apollo has a great sense of what is going on in the world and probably could help me find Murlan. The only problem with that is it's been years since I've been there and I don't know what the best way to get there is."

Lynnaedra put on a face of concern. "The Dragon Slayer Temple? Good luck, Danvel. The past few years it seems like every route to it has encountered some sort of disaster. The Lakes of Astoria have been flooded making them impassable. The Desert of Rebirth has gone completely dark; No sun comes up and no one who has gone in has come out. The Sand Dragons have put up a sandstorm around their territory. The great Golem Sanctuary has been cursed by some sort of petrification; all the Golems have stopped in their tracks and anyone who enters becomes stone themselves. Completely impassable."

"We had planned on visiting it on this trip but it was like a dark force was trying to surround it," Hourig explained.

"What are we going to do?" Gunther asked, taking the biggest drink of his mead yet.

"We don't back down, is what. If we balk at any danger, then we might as well not even go. We face the dangers of the Darkened Desert and don't look back. Every other way is impassable, so that is our route," I said standing and pounding the table with my fist.

Chapter 3 - Hangover? But I Only Had Twenty!

Dragonia

Leviathan Inn

Early Morning

"Wake up, Gunther. Can't get on with an adventure if you spend all day in bed," I said as I picked up the bed he was in and turned it on its side. Gunther fell out with a satisfying thud and groan. Jeff bounded over to the window and opened the curtains, shining the light into the room. Gunther responded with the appropriate hiss.

"How are you not hungover?" Gunther complained as he got up off the floor. He rubbed his head as if he had the worst hangover anyone had ever experienced.

"The real question is how you are! You barely drank a thing," I exclaimed as Gunther rounded the upright bed. That was when I saw the most devastating sight I can remember. "And why the hell are you sleeping naked? I saw my parents die and this is the memory that shall haunt me forever!"

"Neigh! Neigh!" Jeff said as he covered his eyes with the curtains. I feared that Jeff would never be able to see again.

"What? Do you sleep with your armor on?" Gunther asked as he wrapped the blankets around him. It didn't help to lessen the devastation that Jeff and I had felt from seeing what we saw.

"I don't know why you wouldn't. What if something happened while you were sleeping," I said flatly. "I also sleep with my hand on my sword… you know… just in case."

"Just in case what?" Gunther asked as he left the room to get clothed and armored. When he came back in, I pushed the bed over on top of him. "WHAT THE HELL?"

"Just in case… you know…beds fall on you. Meet us in the shops when you get out." Jeff and I ran out of the room and straight out of the inn. The inn had recently won an award from me for having the least original name for an inn.

One thing that most adventurers forgot was the importance of preparation for the adventure. No one ever gets to hear the tale of the adventurer who starved to death because they wouldn't spring for the extra salt cured meat. Those are the people that you see along the road getting eaten by vulture dragons. They are also the people whose skeletons I use to make funny poses for other travelers. Morally unsound? Maybe. Hilarious? Definitely.

Jeff and I took the long way to the shops, passing back through the market. Jeff liberated more apples from the same man's cart as we walked and that's when I saw someone I didn't want to see. The Dragonian training knight was talking to a crowd, his arm in a sling.

As we neared him, it was clear he was telling a tale of a daring adventure from the crowd's reaction. We snaked ourselves through the crowd and positioned ourselves between the two very tall people. From the knight's perspective, he shouldn't have been able to see us.

"... That's when the Behemoth attacked. I don't know if any of you have ever seen a Behemoth before, but there name says it all. As big as the Leviathan Pub and nastier than Leviathan's whirlpools! Tusks as sharp as Gungnir but a wit as dull as Thor's mighty Mjolnir. I saw him lurking on the outside of town and confronted him. Behemoths are notoriously dumb, and this one was exceptionally so. He charged at me and picked me up with his tusks. A normal man would have thought it was over at that point, but I kept a cool head. As he thrashed about I pulled myself up his massive tusk then struck him square in the head, killing him instantly." The crowd responded with roaring applause and cheers. He motioned them to silence and stuck his one good hand on his hip. "I may have broken my hand accomplishing this feat, but you can all rest easy tonight knowing that there are no imminent threats in this vicinity." The crowd began clapping again until a voice rang out from in the middle of them.

"I heard Danvel crushed your hand because you made him angry," The voice yelled above the applause. The applause died down as everyone looked around for the voice. Obviously I had said it, but no one was looking for a pint sized heckler.

"Who said that?" the knight yelled and stepped towards the crowd. "Everyone who didn't say it, get out of the way!" The crowd started to move out of the way, and eventually everyone but Jeff and I (looking suave I might add) had moved out of the way. "Who the hell do you…. uhhh, Oh, Hi, Danvel," the knight said nervously.

I smiled and replied, "Hi. Sorry, I never did get your name." I took a bow and waved for the rest of the townspeople to see me.

"Darren," he answered shortly. The entire crowd was watching the exchange with complete intrigue.

"Nice to meet you, Darren. I'd shake your hand, but I'm afraid I broke it yesterday. Very sorry about that." The crowd erupted in a laughter and ridicule. Phrases like "Behemoth slayer, my ass" and "that knight couldn't even slay a Dragonfly!" rung from the crowd.

Darren dejectedly made his way out of the market. Jeff and I ran after him. "Darren, wait a damn minute."

Darren turned around, face still hanging in embarrassment. "What do you want, Danvel? Haven't you embarrassed me enough today?"

"The only person who did any embarrassing today was you. You embarrassed yourself by lying to all those people. If you want to be a true hero, then you tell the people the truth and show your heroism through your actions. You don't have to lie for people to respect you as a hero, just be one. As a knight you surely have the mettle to do it."

He clenched his one good fist then unclenched. "Thanks for the advice, now get the hell out of my way Dragon Slayer. Some of us have to teach recruits to be knights. And some of us have to do it one handed." And then he was gone.

"Neigh! Neighhh!" Jeff exclaimed. He quickly looked around then chuckled loudly. He was despicable.

"What did I tell you about using that kind of language when there are crowds nearby? But yeah, he was a dick." Jeff responded with a donkey bray. "And an ass, yes. Now let's get to the shops. At this rate, Gunther will have beaten us." We turned back from the market and rushed to the shops.

The shops in Axdremaria harbored the high end merchandise of Dragonia. Rare items, even the occasional items of myth, had passed through these shops. They housed what remained of the Dwarven armor in Dragonia, although they mostly charged exorbitant fees for all of these items. It was the best place to find the uncommon supplies that one might need on an adventure.

We found Gunther in the dressing room... of the tights store. The terror of this morning's sight resurfaced as he came out with a pair of tights on. "What are you doing? We're not shopping for your new underwear! We need to get you new armor," I exclaimed.

"But what's wrong with my armor now? I like it," Gunther replied while dejectedly returning to the fitting room. "Blue just kind of fits me." He exited the fitting room and did his best to look suave in his armor.

"We're going into different territories and we don't need to advertise that we just came from Dragonia. Wyrmvale has allies just like we do. Plus," I said with a wink, "I'm not going to let my squire wear some half rate armor."

"Your squire? Hell yeah!" Gunther cheered. "I'll be the best squire one can be, Mr. Danvel. I promise."

"You'd have to be better than the last one," I said with a snicker. Jeff gave a snort of laughter. "He barely lasted a day."

"So what do I have to do to officially become your squire, Mr. Danvel?" Gunther asked, with pure excitement in his voice.

"First, let's get you some new armor. Then we will procure any supplies need for our adventure. Then we find a mage. Now you might be thinking 'Mr. Danvel, if we can find a mage, then we can get you back to normal.' You probably never realized it because magic isn't a normal part of your life but magic users function in a very serious hierarchy. At the top sits the Grand Wizard, Merlin being the most famous of these. There may be other Grand Wizards but as they are so few and far in between, most don't try and reveal themselves and meddle in history as Merlin has. Below the grand wizard are the Arch-wizards, followed by Elementals, followed by Wizards, then Mages and Healers, and ending with Herbalists. So Mages function at a lower capacity than wizards and often times focus on the transference of magical properties rather than direct spell casting." I finished with a smile, praying that Gunther understood the complexities of what I was saying without me having to get into further detail.

"I get the hierarchy, and I also understand the roles that need to be played out by each rank. Different magics require different skills and different levels of understanding. The only thing I don't get is what we need with a mage," He replied more astutely than I had hoped for. Those days he had spent in the library at the monastery might come in handy on this adventure. Hopefully it would make up for his lack of training and skill.

"A Mage will transfer some of my Dragon Slaying magic into you to help hone your senses and give you a little bit of muscle to help. For the rest? We'll get you a real nice weapon," I said with a keen smile. I didn't want him to feel like I was saying he was useless, but his performance in the arena made me want to be extra prepared in case of battle. "Now let's get over to the Rare Treasure Emporium."

We left the tights store (I flipped a coin to the shop owner for having to deal with Gunther) and went across the brick road to an enormous building. The shop was fairly small, only displaying about twenty items (mostly all of them fake). The real treasures were hidden in a warehouse in the back. Galen Rarefield was what some would call an old friend. They would say that if they didn't know how many times the damn bastard had tried to swindle me. If he wasn't wearing the Green Armor from the Green Knight... If I had any real magic, I'd show him what was what.

Regardless of his chicanery, he still had the best wares on the continent, maybe even in the world. So we entered the building despite my reservations. "Welcome, welcome... Oh, it's you. Stuff's in the back. We got a new shipment with some rare stuff, but knowing you, I'm going to be the one paying." Galen Rarefield wasn't what one would call a thin man. His years of selling overpriced fake merchandise and the occasional real deal had done him well. On his right hand sat Andvaranaut, a ring which produced gold at will, and on his left sat the Ring of Dispel, owned by Lancelot himself, which could dispel any enchantment or curse.

"We'll be putting it on this one's tab if you don't mind," I said as I pointed at Gunther. "We're going on a great adventure and he needs to gear up! So what do you have for us?" Galen bumbled under the counter and activated a magical device which caused the wall behind his counter to disappear. Behind the wall was a warehouse that seemed like it went on for miles. Galen had explained to me once about tesseract magic and a power source of unimaginable power. I think I fell asleep in the middle of the conversation.

"Oh, wow. This play is amazing," Gunther exclaimed. It was akin to seeing a child see his first snowstorm (or in Asgard's case, a child seeing their first Frost Giant).

"Keep your hands to yourself, please. We have a strict, you break it you buy it and you will probably bite it soon because it was most likely cursed policy," Galen said in response to Gunther's excitement. "What type of armament were you thinking of?"

"A hammer," Gunther blurted out. "And I shall smite our enemies like Thor!" He raised his hands and acted like he was joining them together holding Mjolnir.

"Why don't we go with something more long range, Gunther? You remember how things went in the arena. You'd get close enough to hit the Dragon and they'd just sit on you," I said eliciting laughter from Galen and a chuckle from Jeff and Gunther. Gunther then realized I had made fun of him and scowled at me.

"Neighhhh. Neigh, neigh," Jeff said in a more serious tone.

"Jeff is right. You have to think of a weapon and armor that will be easy for you to carry around with you on an extended trip. Why not try a bow and arrow?" Gunther thought on it a minute and nodded his head, yes.

Galen led the way over to a selection of bows. "Here, we have the finest selection of bows in all the lands. First, we have Fail-not. Originally owned by Tristan, it is said to never miss its mark. We don't allow for a field test of this one because we've had one too many revenges acted out while the product hadn't even been purchased." Galen gestured at the rest of the bows.

"Beside Fail-not, we have Eurytus' Bow. Lost to Eurytus after he challenged Apollo, the god, to an archery contest and Apollo killed him; it eventually fell to Odysseus. After Odysseus was done with it… I procured it. A very fine bow. The next one hundred bows were owned by Shiva, Vishnu, Rama, or Karna. What do you think?" Gunther looked over the bows and picked up Eurytus' bow. He grabbed the string and pulled back. What I mean was he tried to pull the string back but it wouldn't budge.

"What gives? This bow is broken," Gunther said, offended by the unbending string. Galen, Jeff, and I fell over with laughter. Gunther stamped his foot and tried again.

"The bow isn't broken, you just aren't strong enough to pull the string," Galen said in between laughs. "I don't usually do this, but try the Fail-not. Hopefully you'll be able to pull back that string." Gunther put back Eurytus' Bow and picked up Fail-not. It was a bow more suitable to his size. Gunther pulled the string back easily and let it go in the most natural set of movements I had seen him make yet.

"I think we have our bow," I said as I gave a Gunther a pat on the back in excitement. Gunther was unprepared and was knocked down two aisles.

Galen hurried after him and said in a cheery tone, "Ah, a shopper at heart. Straight to the quivers because he's quick to buy the match to his new bow." I rolled my eyes and followed. Galen's quiver selection was truly remarkable, if not redundant. Nearly every quiver looked identical but probably had some mystical quality. Or some curse that would've ended up getting us all horribly maimed.

"Do you have any quivers that make it so someone would never accidentally spill all of his arrows out and lose them?" Gunther asked in a shy voice.

"Why, certainly. I have at least fifteen. In which color would you like it," Galen replied, putting on his salesman voice for Gunther. Jeff and I were half asleep with excitement.

"White," Gunther answered. "And some white armor to match." At this point Jeff was asleep and Gunther's reply had woken me up. He seemed to be getting more excited by the minute.

"A man who knows what he wants! Come this way and we shall fit you for the armor." Galen gestured towards further back in the warehouse. Gunther followed quickly. I had less speed as I was dragging a sleeping Jeff behind me. As we finally made it back to the measuring room, we found Gunther looking very uncomfortable as Galen was measuring him. Soon after he was measured, Galen grabbed some armor and placed it on Gunther. "Now, I present… Gunther, the warrior," Galen said in a grand gesture. He'd probably charge us for that, too.

"So how much for all of this?" I asked, waiting for the overpriced merchandise to break my Dragon bank.

"Well, that depends on where you are heading, small Danvel," he said condescendingly. "If you're heading to Wyrmvale, there is a fellow salesman of great rare goods and I have lost a bet to him. If you would deliver him this stone, I would be grateful enough to clear all of your debts." He pulled out a small cloth with a stone inside.

I grabbed the stone, still wrapped in the cloth, from Galen. "So does this thing have any magical properties of which we need to be aware of? We don't need to be in the middle of an adventure and accidentally get blown up."

"Just don't touch it to any lead. Now get out of my store before any other customer shows up and sees that I have actual wares," Galen said as he pushed us out the door. He hated window shoppers. Gunther did really look like a warrior in his new armor and with a bow. A bow which joins the pub and inn by receiving an award for an unoriginal name. Gunther seemed mighty pleased with it as well.

"So where do we find a mage at this time of day? In fact, where do we find a mage at any time of day? I've never met anyone with the ability to harness magic before. Wait a minute, where's

Jeff?" We both looked around to see he was no longer with us and probably still in Galen's warehouse.

I gave a sly smile, "He's probably in there stealing some magical horseshoes or something. I don't know if you've noticed, but Jeff has a problem with stealing things. But he always catches up, usually with something useful. As for the mage, there are several magic stores within Axdremaria. There is also a church nearby which houses mages. So I figure we get something to eat then head to the church. They're more likely to do some charity work for us."

Dragonia

The Church of Christ

Afternoon

Jeff still hadn't made his way back to us by the time we reached the church. A relatively new religion to the area, Christianity was starting to spread like wildfire. For a fairly new structure, it brought memories of the old brilliant architecture which used to decorate the countryside before the war. It was both simplistic and complex at times which brought with it a surprising reverence I hadn't felt in a long time. When we reached the doors of the church, a monk stopped us. "We don't allow any weapons inside the church. Even if you are a Dragon Slayer," the monk said in a soft voice. There was no condescension or annoyance in his voice. Only honesty.

"No problem," we both replied as we gave our weapons for safekeeping. The monk took them and bade us to enter the church. The inside was even more impressive than the outside. The simplicity of the floor layout starkly contrasted the ceiling. On the ground were massive pews and only a small stage for the speaker. The ceiling was adorned with amazing paintings of the heavens and carvings near the tops of the pillars. I assume it was to be symbolic of the glory of the heavens.

"Where do we find a mage in here, then?" Gunther asked in a hushed tone. He must have sensed the feeling of reverence as well.

"I don't know. First time I've been in this church. Probably in the back." We wandered the church for a little searching for the mages and that's when we stumbled upon the garden behind the church. The garden was even larger than the church was and just as magnificent.

Some of these plants didn't exist anywhere except for the Earthwyrm's country. In the middle of the garden were rows of fruits and vegetables and in the center of all those stood a Dragon Fruit cactus. It was more magnificent than any Dragon Fruit cactus I had seen before. Around the massive Dragon Fruit cactus were the mages we were looking for. I assumed it was partly their work that had brought this garden to life as any earth magic or Wyrmvale herbs were forbidden in Dragonia (However, the Baron and Leviathan had come to terms that let holy ground serve as a neutral zone).

I approached the mages and announced myself. "Ho, mages of Dragonia. I am Danvel, the Dragon Slayer, and have come seeking your assistance. I seek to impart my soon to be squire," I gestured to Gunther, "with some of my magical ability so that he may embody a proper squire. Will any of you aid us?" I saw a look of amazement from Gunther and I assume it was for my formal speech. If he only knew it was a load of crap. Getting a mage to help you without them charging you a fee is like getting a Dwarf not to drink on the job… it won't happen.

Only one mage looked over at us and responded. "I, Fandor, shall take on your task Danvel. For free. If this church has taught me anything, it is that we should help one another, fee or no fee. Come; let us go to a more… private part of the garden." Fandor led us to a section of the garden that housed Dragonian native plants.

"Do you have a divining crystal, Danvel? Transfer of this type of magic requires a catalyst. A divining crystal, while rare, is the most common type of catalyst." Gunther and I exchanged glances and a nervous chuckle.

"We were hoping you would happen to have one," I replied. At that very moment Jeff showed up, looking as proper as a Clydesdale on parade day.

"Neigh," He announced in a proud tone and grabbed a crystal from his pack and dropped it on the ground.

"Ah," Fandor said with a smile, "your horse has the crystal." I got up and stood between Fandor and Jeff.

An angry look flashed across Jeff's face, followed by a, "NEIGH!"

"Look at the amount of legs he has, Fandor! Not a horse," I said trying not to upset Jeff. "Let's just get on with this."

Fandor smiled, "Let us indeed. Danvel stand to the left of the crystal and Gunther to the right. The magic shall flow from Danvel to Gunther. In this case it shall grant Gunther some strength and connect you two. Please stay still."

We did as Fandor said and took our positions. His hands rose and the divining crystal rose up between us. Energy shot out of me and then into the crystal then out of the crystal and into Gunther and then it was gone. I felt nothing different but Gunther was knocked back into a bush.

We all rushed over to him and I picked him up off the ground. "Are you alright, Gunther?"

He gave me a half crazed look and said, "I think that fall broke my bush..."

Fandor smiled and gave a quick chuckle, "Well congratulations are in order. You have been imparted with a part of Danvel and are now his squire." There were cheers all around.

"Now to our adventure!"

Chapter 4 - An Adventure Saved is an Adventure Earned

Dragonia

Edge of Axdremaria

The Next Morning

"I told you, you don't have to carry all the supplies," I said, exasperated.

"Neigh!" Jeff replied.

"I never said that! Who said that?! You carry your supplies, I carry mine, and Gunther carries his! That is it," I said throwing his pack at him. He had been going on about it for the last twenty minutes and I was growing more tired of it by the second.

"Neigh," Jeff said with a short snort.

"The same to you, too," I yelled back at him. Gunther walked up to join us. Jeff trotted away sticking his tongue out at me and sneering.

"Can I ask you a serious question, Mr. Danvel? Can you actually understand Jeff?" he asked with a straight face. I was shocked.

"You can't understand him? Don't ever let him know it! If Jeff finds out that you can't understand him, you will never live it down. He's very sensitive about these kinds of things," I explained.

"Can I ask you another question? I've never actually seen you ride Jeff, yet. *Do* you ever ride on him?" He asked with the same straight face. I was completely astonished at the audacity of Gunther's questions.

"What kind of monster are you? Ride my best friend? You really are sick minded. I hope this isn't a side effect of you getting some of my magic because I will take it right back, mister!" I slapped him upside the head and gave him his pack and picked up mine. "Let's move out!"

"I think you are forgetting about your escorts," a voice called from behind us.

"Lynnaedra," I said with genuine cheer in my voice. "What are you and your partners doing here?"

"We thought we would journey with you to the Darkened Sands and then go off on our own adventure. It's just a short distance out of our way. Let's get moving boys," Lynnaedra shouted and then we were off, Hourig and Aturdokht in tow.

Most people assume that the first leg of a journey is an indicator of how the rest of the journey goes. If it starts out smoothly without a hitch, then most likely the rest of the journey should go well. I'm here to tell you that whoever says that most likely has never been on any adventure, or the adventure didn't break out of their home town. Adventures had so many twists and turns that predicting the rest of the journey on the beginning is the way most people get themselves killed.

Dragonia was a country that was renowned for its beautiful cities. Architecture that rivaled the Romans and was sometimes called the next Atlantis. What people didn't notice, though, was that outside of the cities was an awful mess. The countryside was always raining. Lakes and rivers were everywhere you went, so about every mile we either had to find a river crossing or travel around a huge lake. It was one of the most annoying hindrances a travel could run into. While most countries could accurately schedule travel plans, Dragonians just tossed out a month for about everything.

Lynnaedra and Jeff were the only ones enjoying themselves. The two Fire Dragons had left a trail of steam with them since we had left Axdremaria and I wasn't sure if it was because of the rain or the annoyance at all the water. Gunther and I trudged along as best we could. I had the toughest time, getting caught in constant mud holes and unexpectedly getting swept away at a drop in a stream. I felt sort of helpless, but once we got out of this rain I knew I would be fine.

We couldn't start a fire because of all the rain so the Fire Dragons extended their warmth in the rare times that we could find a dry spot. We hypothesized that Leviathan used her powers to keep all the bad weather and unsightly bodies of water away from the major populace so that her cities would stay looking the nicest. Leviathan was called the vainest of all the Dragon Patrons, after all. She apparently liked good appearances.

Because of the conditions, I had warned everyone to be extra careful. Water nymphs, witches, and other types of ill intended creatures used this weather to subdue unsuspecting travelers. Because the land was ever shifting due to the constant water flow, it was hard to track down the creatures and stop them from attacking travelers, fishermen, or the lost. Parents would use these tales to keep children from wandering too far from their towns. There were too many people lost that way.

It was a two day march from Axdremaria to the closest bordee town and so far we had taken three days to get there because of the bad storms and constant stops. Apparently it was rain season, or Leviathan was in a pissy mood to bring such awful storms. We had set up camp early in the morning in a cave we found because the skies were pitch black with a raging storm. Lightning was coming down in almost constant bursts as soon as the storm rolled by.

"Lynnaedra, didn't you feel this storm coming?" I yelled over the thunder that was roaring in the background. It was hard to get a word in with all the thunder. Aturdokht had moved further into the cave to avoid the incoming rain and explore the cave further.

"No, young one. While I can usually feel when a storm of this magnitude is coming, this one just jumped right on us," she roared at me. She was putting on a stoic face but I could tell the storm unsettled her. "I feel like the force that is blocking off the Dragon Slayer Temple has come for us." It wasn't a happy thought. We didn't really know what could be waiting for us if that were true. I found myself clenching my sword handle more often.

"You might be right. The next town puts us a mile or two out from the Darkened Desert. Do you think we should make a run for it? The town can't be much further." At that moment the wind rose up knocking Jeff and I into Hourig. As I felt Jeff slam into me I waited for another thud, but nothing came. I pushed Jeff off me as Hourig gave a mighty harrumph at our crashing into him. I looked around for Gunther but couldn't see him anywhere. "GUNTHER," I yelled out down the cave but nothing came back. Hourig too looked worried. He sent his head back and forth searching for something.

"Aturdokht is gone, too," Hourig's gravelly voice said from behind me. When Hourig finished his sentence, lightning struck nearby sending a blinding flash at us. While I was blinded I felt something grab me. It didn't feel like Gunther's hands or a Dragon's grip so I ripped the arms from the body that housed them (not as easy as I make it sound). A shriek came from the torso and my eyes started to clear. I looked around to find Hourig had dispatched his attacker, too.

"Lightning sprites," I yelled in a rage. "How didn't we see it? It wasn't a water magic storm, it was frickin lightning sprites!" I ripped my sword out and beheaded one trying to run away.

"I'm surprised you even know what they are, Danvel. Such a rare creature. It was easier to believe a dark force at work rather than miscreant sprites," Hourig said as he dug his claws into the one I had disarmed. "Lynnaedra is gone now, as well. Where have you taken them, sprite?" the Dragon roared. While I had heard Lynnaedra's roar before, Hourig was something else entirely. Truly a fierce creature. I scanned the area to see that Jeff was gone.

"Hock dank sha tsch, PAHCK," the sprite replied. Hourig dug his claws in deeper drawing what one could assume was blood.

"English, if you would, sprite," Hourig growled. His back started to spit massive amounts of smoke from it from his anger.

The creature cried in pain from Hourig's claws, but eventually answered. "In the back of the cave, you filthy serpent." Hourig responded by removing its head from its body.

"They took our supplies, too. Why do all the mischievous creatures always have to steal supplies? Supplies cost money, and I'm hungry," I said as we started into the cave. Hourig used his inner fire to light up the cave the further we got in. It also made things very toasty.

"We have more important things to worry about than our supplies, Danvel. Our friends need us," Hourig said hurrying his pace. I matched his speed.

"But, if we rescue our friends and there's nothing to eat, then they die a slow agonizing death instead of instant death. Also, I'm hungry," I said drawing my sword. A faint buzzing noise started to arise from further down the tunnel. "Dim your light, Hourig. Perhaps we can catch them by surprise." As Hourig dimmed his inner flame as we rushed forward, but we weren't prepared for the scene we encountered.

In the corner lay Gunther, Lynnaedra, and Aturdokht, all unconscious. Jeff, however, was not only awake, but had slain all the remaining lightning sprites. All fifty lightning sprites. The horrifying sight was that he was eating all of my food!!!

"By Fafnir's beard. Danvel, your companion is unbelievable. To slay fifty lightning sprites on his own," Hourig said in amazement. It really was an uncanny feat. And he wasn't even drunk this time!

"Yeah, people tend to underestimate him and his fighting ability," I replied as I slapped his mouth away from my pack. "That is my food and you know it, Jeff. First, you complain about having to carry packs I didn't say you had to carry and NOW you eat MY food!" I yelled. "He killed them all just because he was hungry, you know."

"Neighhhhhhhhhhh," Jeff whined. He got up and pathetically walked over to his own pack.

"Let us gather our friends and leave this wretched place," Hourig interjected to move along the pace. He roused Lynnaedra and Aturdokht to their senses and soon their supplies and packs were collected. Gunther would not rise, however. I threw him over

Lynnaedra's shoulder while Jeff grabbed his pack and we followed the Dragon trio out. When we got outside, the lightning storm was still raging and lightning was coming down more frequently than before.

"I thought that killing the lightning sprites would have stopped the storm," Aturdokht yelled above the lightning strikes. I could barely hear him. The constant barrage of sounds was starting to become too much.

"I think we just pissed off their master, is all," I said as I drew my sword, keeping it low as not to draw attraction from the lightning. That's when the lightning began to converge on the cave and it exploded revealing three giant Raiju in the shape of wolves. There stood a wizard in between them all.

"Who has disgraced this cave and killed my servants?" The wizard called out to our group. I responded by throwing my sword at the nearest Raiju and striking it in the head. The monster fell backwards in pain but rose again, my sword passing through it. The Raiju responded by shooting lightning from its tail at me. Hourig jumped in front of me, blocking the blast.

"They are creatures of pure lightning, Danvel. We need magic to defeat them, or to defeat the wizard," Hourig explained. "Lynnaedra, get the team out of here while Danvel and I deal with these vermin." Lynnaedra nodded her head, picked up Gunther and ran the opposite way with Aturdokht. Jeff stayed behind as I expected he would. As the three left, the wizard lifted his staff into the air and struck the ground hard. The Raiju responded by leaping forward at us and lightning began striking the ground around the wizard, making it nearly impossible for anyone to get near him.

Hourig grabbed one of the Raiju with his mouth and slammed it to the ground while Jeff squared off to face one. The last Raiju, the one I had thrown my sword at began running circles around me getting faster by the second. Soon it was only a blur of the lightning it was made from. Then it was on me. And it hurt like hell. Even though I had my armor on, the bites of the Raiju sent electric shocks through my whole body and every time I tried to punch it, it shocked me. If only I could get to my sword.

As the Raiju bit and clawed at me, I stubbornly stood up and slammed it to the ground. The wind, or whatever it had, was knocked out for a moment, allowing me to break free. I took a moment to survey the scene. Hourig was successfully fending off his Raiju and Jeff seemed to be faring the same as I was. Then I made a dash for my sword. It didn't go unnoticed. The wizard struck his staff to the ground twice and lightning began to pour down around my sword and along the path to it.

As I juked and jived out of the lightning's path I began to lose speed, allowing my Raiju to catch up to me. Then it was on top of me again. As I put my hands up to defend myself, I noticed Jeff was in the exact same position as me and more Raiju had been summoned to battle Hourig. The first battle in our adventure was going poorly. That was when in between all the sounds of battle and the lightning striking I heard a faint thwip and a low whistle. At nearly the same time I heard the thud, the Raiju was off of me and sitting on the ground beside me and the lightning had stopped striking.

When I looked over to where the magician had been standing, there was a crumpled body with an arrow sticking out of his head. About fifty yards back, Gunther stood with his bow at his side. The black clouds turned back to the white grey they had been the whole time previously on the journey. When my vision returned to the Raiju, its form had changed to a fox. It looked actually quite pleasant.

"We're terribly sorry to inconvenience you and your travel party. We were enslaved by that rotten wizard there and unable to roam the frequent storms of the Dragonian countryside like we are so accustomed to doing. Thank you for freeing us," the fox Raiju said in a kind manner. "My brothers have already risen to the clouds to join their families and once again roam, but I could not leave without giving you a reward." The group stood in a stunned kind of silence until I spoke up.

"We are glad that we were able to unintentionally free you from enslavement, Fox. But what could you offer us?" I asked trying to emulate the kind manner that he provided us with. It was the least I could do considering we were just fighting to the death.

"During the storms, the Raiju overheard your desires to go into the Darkened Desert. So I shall accompany you by merging with your sword and become your companion. It is the least I can do," the fox Raiju said, once again in a most polite manner.

"I don't think I could say no to that. The more the merrier... as long as you don't need to eat any of our food," I responded with a quick smile and held out my sword. The fox Raiju touched his paw

to the sword, causing a blinding light to shoot out. When our vision

cleared up I looked up and saw that my sword was no longer

completely black. Streaks of lightning periodically shimmered in it

and the edge of the blade now shone completely white.

"Let us join Lynnaedra and Aturdokht. They're sure to be

worried since they were too afraid to join the glory of battle," Hourig

said with a wink as he turned towards Earwyna, the nearest town. He

tried to play it cool but I knew he was secretly jealous of my

lightning sword thing. I went over to Jeff to make sure he was okay

only to find him pouting.

"What's the matter, buddy? Mad that Gunther's the big hero

and not you?" I asked in a semi mocking tone.

"Neigh Neigh Whinny Neigh Neighhhhh," Jeff replied with a

pouty tone. He kicked his feet in the air and sighed.

"No, I don't know why the Raiju didn't merge with your

horseshoes and let you have cool new ones," I said, placing my

hands on his face. "Your horseshoes are Asgardian and some of the

strongest in the world. You don't need new ones." Why did my best

friend have to be so whiny? I pulled Jeff to his hooves and pointed for him to follow Hourig. I went over to the now dead wizard and Gunther standing over him.

"I've never killed a man before, Mr. Danvel. Never killed anything actually. I don't know how to feel about it. We're barely at the beginning of this quest of self-discovery and I've already taken a life," he said with a tear forming in his eye. "What does this mean about who I am?"

"I'll tell you the only thing it means to me. It means you are willing to do whatever it takes to save your friends and that you are willing to strike down evil when it comes at us. I couldn't ask for a better companion on this trip. Well you know, except Jeff," I said with a wink. "Remember what Hourig said. 'Quests of self-discovery often lead us where we least expect.'" I patted his back once and started off to follow the rest of the group.

Gunther trailed behind us the rest of the trip. No one talked about it because we all knew there was nothing to say. Gunther was going to have to decide what this meant all by himself and decide how it would shape who he wanted to be. In a few short hours, we reached Earwyna and met with Lynnaedra and Aturdokht.

It was one of the happiest moments of the trip. No rain and sunny skies. Earwyna was about two miles from the edge of the Darkened Desert and unless you were blind, you would see why it had been renamed that. There was sunshine all around until you looked at the area that the desert started. It looked like a starless night.

The town was supposed to be one of the most heavily populated border towns in the continent but there wasn't a soul to be seen. Even the fountains seemed to only sputter water out, as if the water was afraid of the darkness.

"Most of the townspeople have left the town for fear of the darkness spreading," Lynnaedra explained. "Even more left when that wizard showed up on the other side of town. There are only a few families left. I've talked with Aturdokht, and I think we are going to stay in this town for a little bit." Hourig grumbled at this and walked away in a huff mumbling something about feeling more alive than he has in fifty years.

"So it's goodbye, then," I said with a soft smile. "I hope your stay is better than the beginning of our adventure, Lynnaedra."

"And I hope your adventure is better than it's beginning, Danvel. Gunther," she said getting his attention, "do not strain too much on what you've done. We are all tasked to do things we aren't ready for and things we should never have to do. You have faced both of these and are still standing. Move forward and discover who you are." Gunther didn't reply. Then she turned to Jeff. "Jeff, you stallion. Take care of these haphazard men. They are sure to find more danger than they can expect to cope with. Goodbye all.

Aturdokht came behind her and took a bow, maintaining his quiet personality. "GET THE HELL OUT OF HERE," Hourig yelled from some unknown place. It was a quiet goodbye. The best kind of goodbye.

"Are we ready for the next leg of our journey?" I asked, focusing on Gunther particularly.

"Neighhhh," Jeff replied in affirmative.

"Can't get anywhere standing here, can we?" Gunther said half-heartedly. At least he was trying.

Chapter 5 - The Behemoth Trials

Border of Dragonia/ The Darkened Desert

Midday

"So do we just walk into the darkness?" I asked, stumped by the unnatural representation of the border. You could see the moon shining in the sky in front of us and feel the sun beating down behind us. The border extended as far as the eye could see. I didn't like it.

"What if that is what is killing the adventurers?" Gunther retorted. "Could be that no one reports back about what's happening there because they are all dead." So I pushed him in. "What the hell?" he yelled. "You could have killed me!"

"Lesson one as my squire: Death can happen at any time. Be prepared. There are no Dragons here to protect us anymore so we have to be ready to fight at a moment's notice." I helped him off the ground after Jeff and I stepped into the darkness with Gunther. As soon as we entered, Jeff pretended he was dying. It was a beautiful bit of acting.

"Ha ha. Very funny, Jeff," Gunther said sarcastically. "Can we just get moving?"

"Lesson number two: Survey your surroundings before moving forward. We're in a new environment that presents new challenges. We can barely even see in front of us." That's when an unexpected surprise came.

"I believe I can be of some assistance," a voice came from nowhere in particular. We all looked stupefied.

"Fox, is that you?" I called out. "Wait, what do we call you?" That's when the fox Raiju shot out from my sword and appeared in front of us.

"Fox will be fine. I believe I can shed some light in this world." Fox demonstrated by illuminating our surroundings. "It was getting stuffy in that sword anyways."

I smiled and motioned us all forward. The most jarring part of the desert wasn't that there were no stars in the sky. It was the massive moon. Everywhere you looked it felt like it was in your view. It was even scarier that it barely gave off any light. It was like there was a fog of darkness surrounding every light source. I was half worried that the air might be toxic.

Another problem was direction. Without any stars, it was hard to tell if we were continuing in a straight line or not. The desert offered no real landmarks and since we couldn't see more than ten feet in front of us, they would have been useless anyhow. We aimlessly wandered around hoping that the next dune would give us some answers.

The biggest problem was the cold. We hadn't thought that the dayless desert would be so frigid so Fox was continually shocking the three of us to keep us moving. We didn't want to use fires too often in case someone was lurking out in the desert. The sand didn't help either. Constantly getting into our armor and packs.

It wasn't till about the fifth day (I assume since there was no real way to tell) that we started to feel that something was nearing us. Our hairs were standing on edge with anticipation hoping to find an end to all of this misery.

"I think I saw a hulking shadow out on the edge of Fox's glow," Gunther said, warming himself on the fire. We had broken down and decided to take an extended rest to try to warm ourselves and our armor before moving forward.

"Definitely is something out there. Jeff can smell it," I replied. Jeff had been circling the fire in time with the shadow. "I think it's been following us for a day or so. Pretty sure it's a Behemoth." Jeff continued his circling, never looking at the fire.

Gunther had a worried look on his face. "A Behemoth? How will we face that? I've read that they can become bigger than castles!" Gunther started to panic and picked up his bow. I had never seen the kid more nervous than that moment.

"Put your damn bow down, Gunther. Your books must not be worth much if they don't give you any more than that about Behemoths. Nomadic tribe. Bigger than most Dragons and older, too. Most important information that most people seem to gleam over is that they are a tribe of scholars. They travel from library to library to get knowledge. Crossing continents and oceans just to read. I'd be panicked too if I were you, Gunther. They might actually know something that you think you know," I said laughing. Jeff joined in the laughter, too. Even Fox let out a hefty chuckle.

Then a disturbing thing happened. The Behemoth outside our camp started laughing as well. "Danvel, you are as sharp-witted as ever and at only half the size," He bellowed. That was when he entered the illumination radius of the fire and Fox. Truth be told, as much as I knew about Behemoths and having encountered them several times; they were damn frightening at times. He was nearly ten times taller than me and even though his face was over our fire, I couldn't see his end.

He had tusks that extended close to ten feet and a beard that stayed close to his chin. Intimidating, sure, but I'd recognize that face anywhere. "By the lack of stars, Bernard? Bernard is that you?"

I exclaimed. When I was a fledgling Dragon Slayer I happened upon the tribe of Behemoths and tried to fight with them. Bernard was the Behemoth that took pity enough to set me aside and teach me about things other than Dragons. He also stopped the Behemoths from killing me.

"I ne'er thought we would have the chance to see each other again," Bernard said extending a hand... paw... whatever they were outward towards me. I shook his hand and gave him a high five (yes, I was the one who invented them). "Just as strong as e'er, too. You're a wee bit smaller than I remember, though. Did you catch some of that reverse aging that Merlin has?" As our conversation continued I noticed that Gunther, Jeff, and Fox were giving us both strange looks. Gunther still had his hand clutched around his bow.

"It is a long story, Bernard. But I seem to have forgotten to introduce my companions, strange as they be. My loyal steed, Jeff. My squire, Gunther. And my brand new companion, Fox, the Raiju." I allowed pleasantries to flow between the strangers before continuing my conversation with Bernard. I filled him in on what had happened with Murlan and our quest of self-discovery. Bernard listened with intent until I was finished with my tale. Even after I finished he stayed silent for a long time.

"Tis a strange thing for Murlan to have cast such a curse on you and then to run. Perhaps he had miscast the spell and didn't want to stick around for the wrath of the angry Danvel. Tis even stranger, these tales about the Dragon Slayer Temple being cut off from the rest of the world. I had no knowledge that the Sand Dragons had shut off their land from outsiders and that the Lakes of Astoria had flooded. It seems unusual that they would be so flooded during their dry season. And the fate of the great Golems. Such wonderful and creative creatures. As well as what has befallen here…," Bernard made a strange face as he said this.

"So you know what has happened to the Desert of Rebirth, Bernard?" Gunther spoke up, breaking out of his trance of awe.

"Not just what has befallen the Desert, young Gunther, but has befallen our tribe. Something has happened to the King and has left us to wander this desert searching for a way to help him," Bernard said in a worried voice. The Behemoth King was one of the oldest creatures on the planet and had one of the biggest compendiums of knowledge, ever. To have him silenced would be to take a great unknown treasure out of the world.

"What happened to the King?" I said, rising and putting my armor on so I could go help.

"Stay your haste, Danvel and let me explain. When we entered the desert, the King began his trek for the Phoenix as he always does. The Phoenix imparts his feathers to our tribe as we pass knowledge to him about the goings on of the world. The King didn't make it far before a knight in cerulean armor came and struck our fair monarch in the head with a blade. The blade bonded with our King and then the changes came. Darkness came over the desert and our King became a cruel tyrant."

I continued putting on my armor as I replied, "Then let's go pull that sucker from his head!" Jeff neighed in agreeance and Gunther had a look of semi terror on his face.

"You presume we didn't try this, Danvel. We are smart creatures, no? That was when the first Behemoth died. As soon as she touched the blade, her body shriveled away. We began to throw items at our King to see what could affect the sword. Nearly everything disintegrated once it touched it. They only thing that survived was our Dimitrios Ore."

"Is your King killing all the adventurers who pass through here?" Gunther interjected.

"At first, yes. He claimed the desert as his own and started executing what he called trespassers. After his first few executions, I started lurking at the edge of the desert to help the travelers. We have hidden them in a cave that leads deep within the sand and they are helping us with how to fix our king. As we are merely scholars and aren't very adept at hard work, we couldn't do anything with the Dimitrios Ore. We began using the adventurers to forge a sheath and glove of the Dimitrios ore. They accomplished this task, but then we had another problem. No regular human could stand against the might of the Behemoth King. Ten died in attempts before we decided that it was no longer an option."

"But then I wandered in," I came back. "Me and my team that is. We have the advantage of numbers and magic." Bernard thought on this for a long time. As Bernard pondered my "offer" Gunther pulled me over to the rest of the team.

"What do you mean by magic, Mr. Danvel?" He asked. The looks on everyone else's faces told me they would like an explanation as well, although who knew what Fox's facial expression really meant?

"So you know how, generally, the sentient beings on this planet are five to one hundred percent magical? Fox is eighty to ninety percent magic, that's why he doesn't have much of a corporeal form. Jeff is about twenty percent magical. He was divined by magical means and most Asgardian things fall under that percentage. Humans are generally five percent magic. Because I'm a Dragon Slayer, I'm around ten percent. Behemoths have no magic at all. It's why they live so long; it's why they seek knowledge of the earth. It's why they grow so big. In the same manner, it's why one hundred percent magical creatures are so huge and seek magical knowledge."

"So if we attack the Behemoth King with magic, it will kill him?" Gunther asked in a semi confused tone.

"No," Bernard answered. "Only a physical attack or incredibly powerful magical attack can kill a one hundred percent physical being. It means that the King can't harm the magical creature and is more susceptible to magical manipulation. I agree that it is our best option."

"Then it is settled. We're going to save a king," I replied throwing my fist in the air. Everyone looked at me like I was insane. "Let's just get going!"

Bernard led the group to a set of caves nearly a day (once again, I am assuming) from where we had been. The cave we entered was barely big enough to allow Bernard entrance, but somehow he fit inside. We continued down into the caves until we found what I could only describe as a small village of people living inside. Houses, a stable, and some farm animals all crammed inside the cave. Among the houses was a blacksmith, although how they were venting the smoke created was unknown to me.

The houses themselves were rudimentary and I assume built with whatever supplies Bernard could sneak away from the Behemoth tribe. A piece of tent cloth for a roof. Some rocks from the caves as support beams. It was both sad and amazing. Sad because of the conditions they were living in. Amazing that the people from all different walks of life seemed to be thriving in it.

"So what properties does the Dimitrios Ore hold that stops the sword's magic?" Fox asked. It was surprising to see him talk directly to anyone else since he mostly had only acknowledged me. I was also surprised at how easily everyone had taken to a mostly non corporeal being in our group. I thought for sure Jeff wouldn't have accepted it. Damned bigoted Sleipnir.

"We aren't sure exactly," Bernard replied. "Dimitrios Ore is some of the rarest and oldest type of ore in the world. It may have magical properties that haven't been explored yet because of its rarity. We barely had enough to make the items to do our experiment with the sword let alone test its magical properties."

"Bernard! You've returned with more strangers and unharmed. Tis a good sign," someone called out from the smithy. A Behemoth the size of a small Dragon charged out and plowed directly into Bernard.

"Son! It is good to see you too." The two Behemoths embraced. It was a heartwarming sight in the face off all that seemed to be going wrong for the Behemoths and our fellow adventurers.

"What kind of kid calls their dad by their name?" Gunther asked me, elbowing me to get my attention. For some reason he forgot I had armor on and began rubbing his elbow.

Bernard turned his attention toward us. "The kind that is seventy-five years old, young Gunther. Meet my son, Benedict. We also have exceptional hearing. The Behemoth I told you about who touched the sword in the King's head was my wife, his mother. So please Danvel, do your best to stop the King and the sword." Bernard hugged his son again after pleading with me.

"Well let's see this Dimitrios sheath and glove then," I urged on. Benedict led the group into the smithy's workplace (Bernard couldn't fit anything but his head in). The blacksmith was working on the anvil when Benedict ran up to him called his name. Calling it a workplace was an overstatement, though. There was only three or so tools, and metal strewn about the place.

"Alabaster! Bernard has returned with more people!" Benedict announced excitedly.

"Oi, we don't need any more people here! What we need is someone who can stand up to the King and actually pull this off!"

He turned back to his anvil and continued working, ignoring our presence.

"What you need is me," I interjected. "I'm Danvel, Dragon Slayer extraordinaire. Pleased to make your acquaintance," I said with my cockiest smile. Jeff hid his face and Gunther just shook his head at what I said. "Can I see the glove and sheath?" Bernard nodded his head to signal this was okay.

"Whatever ye say Bernard, but I think Dragon Slayers are a bunch of crap made up from old tales," Alabaster replied. He brought over the glove and sheath and handed them to me. Like my armor it was black, but unlike my armor no light seemed to reflect off of it; there was no shine despite being close to a fire. I then grabbed Alabaster by his shirt and hung him on a nearby rung for tools.

"Yes, we Dragon Slayers don't exist at all. No enhanced strength or anything. Surely a bunch of crap." This drew a chuckle from everyone except Alabaster. Then I tried on the glove. "Perfect fit," I exclaimed. "The sheath seems a little short, though," I said as I examined it. "Are we sure it will be able to contain it?"

"We did the best with what we had... Dragon Slayer," Alabaster replied. I picked him up and put him back on the ground. He went back to his anvil and angrily beat at the piece of metal he was working on.

"So what is the plan?" Fox asked. Even though I had explained about magical properties, I didn't explain how it was relevant to any plan of action.

"Pretty simple actually. Bernard smuggles us in, Fox and Jeff distract the Behemoth King, and I climb the King and tear out the sword. Simple." The reaction that I got from everyone was that they thought it was anything but simple.

"What will I be doing?" Gunther asked softly and I believe a little bit sadly.

"You get the hard task. If all things fail, you shoot. Whether it is the King... or me. We don't know if the glove will work, and we need an insurance policy." This elicited a large argument between the groups. Bernard and Benedict were completely against the idea of killing the King. Jeff was outraged at the potential of my death. Alabaster was arguing that we should just kill the King and not even risk others' lives if we have the chance. Gunther sort of sunk back and out of the room. Fox was just watching everyone quizzically.

"Silence!" I yelled. "I understand your concerns but we need to be realistic. Bernard and Benedict: I don't want to kill the King either, but if this doesn't work, we can't allow the dark magic to spread or allow him to keep killing. We also can't keep all these people here indefinitely. Jeff: I don't want to die! I never want to die, but let's say that the sword takes over my brain and warps me somehow. Do you really want a crazy super-strengthened midget running around? Alabaster: Shut up." The crowd fell quiet.

"Danvel is right, we need to take every precaution, regardless of our feelings," Bernard said. The other didn't seem to want to hear it, but said it was.

"Neighhhhh," Jeff said sadly.

"I know, young Sleipnir. Everything carries with it great risk, some things more than others." The rest of the group now discussed the plan in a less volatile manner.

I slipped out from among them to go find Gunther. It didn't take long to find him on the edge of the village staring into the dark black of the cave. "I know it's a heavy burden I've laid upon you,

Gunther. If there were any other way, I'd choose it, but you were the one who had to pick a bow that never misses," I said as I laid a playful punch on his shoulder.

"I just don't know if I'm cut out for this kind of thing, Mr. Danvel. I've seen more action and terrors in the past week and a half than I ever read about in my books. I don't know if I'm going to end up being the man I want to be; A hero." Gunther put his head into his hands and began to sob.

"Let me tell you a few things I've learned about being a hero that those books will never tell, Gunther. A hero isn't some knight in shining armor, although having shining armor is great. A hero is someone who is going to go out and make the decisions that other people either can't or won't make. Do you think it's easy to kill Dragons? Most Dragons I kill have family members and friends who care about them. But those people who care about them don't want to have to make that hard decision themselves. They'd rather set it upon some guy who has a neat title and has inherited magic from his bloodline. And they never appreciate the burden I've taken from them. No, I end up being the guy who took away their loved one. I have to live with their burdens and that's why they call me a hero. So

I'm asking you to take this decision from the Behemoths and from anyone who cares about me, Gunther. I'm asking you to be their hero," I finished by extending my hand towards him.

"I'll do it," he replied as he we shook hands. I lifted him off his feet and we joined the others.

"Have we all settled our squabbles then?" I asked as we walked in.

"I believe so," Bernard answered.

"Then let's get some sleep, we have a big day tomorrow."

Chapter 6 - Phoenix on the Rise

Darkened Desert

The Cave Town

Who the Hell Knows?

"Everyone get a good perpetual night's sleep?" I asked to all the sleepy eyed crew. Despite everyone else falling asleep, I had snuck out of the village and was watching the moon most of the night. I was never good at sleeping the night before I had to do dangerous work. Dangerous work that might get me killed, that is. The crew all looked like they had had restless nights except for Fox... he just looked like a fox... of lightning.

Bernard and Benedict hurriedly raced down the cave. "We must evacuate the caves immediately! Behemoths loyal to the dark King are coming this way. Danvel's group must come with me and the rest of you go with Benedict. He will lead you to the border that I am supposed to be guarding."

We hurried along and said goodbyes and thank yous to whoever needed it. Bernard and Benedict said a longer goodbye than everyone else but separated in a hurried fashion. We followed Bernard straight out of the caves and didn't stop. Not even when we heard the group of Behemoths behind us. Not even when we heard the screams behind us. I could feel Bernard's pace slow for just a second and then resume.

When we were safely beyond the sounds of fighting we stopped to catch our breath. "We should have gone back," Gunther said, feeling guilty. We all felt guilty. Even I wanted to go back and help them but knew we couldn't.

"No," Bernard exclaimed. "We all knew the risks. If we had gone back then we would never be able to save the King and this would all have been for naught. Plus the loyal members would have known I was acting against the King's' interests and I would never be able to sneak you in."

We continued the rest of the way in silence and in almost utter darkness. Fox hid in my sword and we all held onto Bernard as we moved forward. Behemoths must be able to see in darkness or he was using his memory to find our way back. Soon we were able to see the fires of the Behemoth camp and our pace slowed to a near halt. "I shall distract the majority of the camp and the rest of you must stay low and sneak in. The King never takes notice unless directly spoken to. Do not make a sound or they will hear you. Good luck." Then Bernard moved towards the camp, leaving us behind.

We went towards the camp at a different angle, trying to avoid the torches. Soon we heard the calls of Bernard. "Great King! Great King! A massive army approaches from my section of the border. I would've tried to eliminate them myself but the army was more massive than I could handle alone. Let me take the guard and hurry to meet them!" The guard all moved forward to meet Bernard.

There were almost twenty in the group. More than enough to take down most armies.

The King spoke in a grave voice. "Guard, go with him. Kill every single one of them. Show those fools no mercy!" Bernard led the guards out of the camp and beyond our line of sight. We waited for a few minutes after to ensure they were out of hearing distance.

The camp was nearly empty except for two of the royal guards and the King himself. We snuck into one of the massive tents and all huddled around. I pulled out my sword and whispered. "Fox, get rid of the guards." Fox jumped from out of the sword and then out of the tent in one hop. We all crowded around the entrance as we watched him… or her… whatever, jump around quick as lightning in front of the guards and the King.

"Kill it, you fools!" The King exclaimed. In the flashes of Fox's lightning, we could see the dark energy that the sword was permeating from the behemoth King's head. It was even darker than the starless night in the desert. Just looking at it, you could feel the malice from it. The guards chased after Fox out of the camp and beyond our sight.

I pulled Jeff and Gunther close and whispered. "Jeff, I want you to go up and kick him right in the nose and run. Gunther, stay in here and have your arrow ready." I pulled the glove on and smiled. "I'm going to pull the sword from the King!" I dashed out of the tent and looked over to Jeff who was running full speed at the King. I reached the King's tail at the same time Jeff kicked him; I could see him recoil in shock.

"What atrocity is this?" the King roared. "I am the King of all knowledge! The Behemoth King. A SLEIPNIR DARES STRIKE ME?" I responded by climbing as fast I could up his back. It wasn't easy. He was writhing back and forth in anger and his fur wasn't conducive to climbing, but still I tried. When I reached about halfway up him, I saw a light flashing and saw Fox flying around in front of the King. The King then stood up in a furor and roared. The thrashing he then began didn't help my ascent either. Soon I was holding on for dear life. I could tell that Fox was leading them all on a merry chase and that Jeff was showing up in between to keep the King distracted, but I couldn't tell if he was totally aware of my presence.

Despite all of the thrashing about, I finally made it up to the shoulder blades and saw the sword. Regardless of the lack of light and the dark energy it was producing, I could see it clear as day; even the part of the sword that was buried in the King's cranium. It was a beautiful katana, both simple and elegant. A true masterpiece of craftsmanship and sorcery. Then Fox came up and slammed into the King, causing him to rear up. I grabbed the sword with my gloved hand and held on for dear life. The sword and King recoiled at this. The King responded by speaking in a language I didn't understand and smashing into tents. The sword responded by shooting bolts of dark energy out, which destroyed anything it touched.

Then a bolt of energy struck Gunther's tent, disintegrating it and leaving Gunther coverless. Gunther was also knocked back by the force of the blast. I knew I had to end this now, so I pulled my own sword out with my free hand, stabbed it into my colossal opponent, and used it as leverage to pull the dark blade free from the King. After four or five pulls, I wrenched it free from his skull and shoved it in the sheath. The King fell to the ground immediately and the night was gone, revealing a bright desert sky. I was blinded instantly and thrown from the King. I felt Jeff and Fox come to my side and carry me off.

When my eyes finally adjusted, I was shocked at what I saw. The two royal guards had been struck by the dark energy and were dying in front of us. The King lay unconscious with my sword sticking out of his head. Many of the women and children Behemoth were surrounding him. Most of the camp had been destroyed.

Jeff was pulling Gunther, who was howling in pain, over to us when the Behemoths who were not in the royal camp saw us. "Murderers! They've killed our King." They began charging at us when an unfamiliar voice spoke up.

"Hold your accusations, fair ladies. For Danvel and his company hath not slain your King but saved him from a wretched fate. However, Danvel, could you please come retrieve your sword? I've had that other one in my head for so long I could do with a break." I complied with the King's request as he gave instructions to the women and children. He sent the children to go retrieve every Behemoth, hopefully before any more bloodshed had been wrought, and the women were to help repair the camp.

I checked on my team as the Behemoths took their orders. Jeff and Fox were completely okay, but Gunther had received a large amount of damage to his arm from the dark energy. The cut was down to the bone. We tried to calm him and stop the bleeding, but to our dismay, there was none. The dark energy somehow cauterized the wound with energy. "Mr. Danvel, it hurts so much," He screamed.

The King noticed and rushed over. "Pack sand on his wound and cover it. These are the sands of the Phoenix, so they have magical restorative properties." We did as quickly as we could and then covered his wound. By the time we were finished, Gunther was passed out.

"Thank you, King," I exclaimed, as I laid Gunther down.

"No. Thank you, Danvel. You have saved me and my people from a terrible fate. My thoughts were clouded with a deep hatred and I wasn't myself. I fear that our once peaceful race will now become exiled by all who hear," the King said as he started to walk away. He walked at a slow pace, clearly meaning for me to follow.

I motioned for Fox and Jeff to stay with Gunther and ran after the King. "How did this all happen? I can hardly imagine you just happened to fall head first onto a sword."

The King stopped for a second and then continued walking. "A knight in cerulean appeared to us as a friend. He did not say his name or where he was from, but presented the sword to us asking its origins. When no one else could identify it, I was recalled from my journey. I was on my way to see the Phoenix but turned around straightaway. Can you blame me? You know how important knowledge is to us. As I went to examine this newly discovered katana, the man in cerulean stuck the blade straight into my head. Within seconds he was missing and the sky started to turn black. And then my thoughts turned to black, too. I can remember everything that happened, but for the life of me I cannot think of why I would have let them happen. I have killed so many."

I gave the King a good pat on his leg. "It's not your fault, King. Do you feel like Dragonia perpetrated this? Cerulean armor is their calling card." I didn't think that Dragonia would do such a thing, especially unprovoked. Dragonia didn't even fight back when Wyrmvale initiated the new war.

"It is hard to tell in times of war like this, Danvel. It could have easily been a member of Wyrmvale trying to pit us against Dragonia. I feel that once we locate the Phoenix, my people will head northward and strafe the border between Dragonia and Drakeland. There is much to be learned along this border of water and wind. If you have need of us, Danvel, you may call us to your aid anytime. For now, however, I feel I must rest. Two blades to the head are enough to slow even one such as I. When a tent is erected, your people may rest in it."

I returned to the team and sat down. No one spoke as the Behemoths worked around us. Then I took a look at the sheath. As I had feared, it was too short and a small bit of the sword was left exposed. I covered it with some cloth of a ripped tent and put it in with my supplies. Then I fell asleep.

Desert of Rebirth

Behemoth Camp

Night

I was disconcerted by how fast I had become accustomed to waking up with the sky pitch black. I was also disconcerted that I was so worn out that I didn't notice that someone moved me. I called for Fox and he appeared from my sword, giving off a faint light. Gunther was lying beside me, still passed out and Jeff was nearby, snoring as loud as could be. Sometimes I wondered if he was really sleeping or just pretending so he could annoy me.

"What is it, sir?" he asked in his ever so polite manner.

"What did I miss while I was asleep?" I asked as I rubbed the sleep from my eyes.

"Much has happened. The Behemoth King went alone on his journey and the Behemoths rebuilt much of their camp. Then several of them left to scour for survivors of the affair; Behemoths that left the tribe, humanoids that survived the attacks... There are only four left in the camp at the moment. Two guards to protect us in case someone were to attack, Bernard, and Benedict. Benedict is in bad shape, though. When he was caught leading the humanoids away, his fellow Behemoths were brutal. He and Alabaster fought against five Behemoths and gave everyone else time to escape."

"What happened to Alabaster?" I said in a soft tone.

"He died, slaying a Behemoth by himself," Bernard said from outside the tent. "A feat that some would call impossible." He peered his head in. "Come walk with me, Danvel."

Fox and I both went out, nodding at the guards, and followed Bernard. He led us to his tent where Benedict lay. Both of his tusks had been crushed, and one of his legs looked beyond repair. "When the King saw the extent of his injuries, he left immediately to find the Phoenix. I fear he will not make it in time though. Despite his size and youth, he was able to take down two of the Behemoths before the last two killed Alabaster and descended upon him. Alabaster's name shall go down in our history books as a true hero."

"I'm sorry, Bernard," I said laying my hand on him. It was hard to show true comfort to a Behemoth. They were so damned tall. Regardless, Bernard understood the sentiment.

"You have nothing to be sorry for, Danvel. Only with the perpetrator of the initial act of violence lays the blame. Even the King holds no blame in this, though it was his order to show no mercy," he said with a bitter tone. His logical side was saying the words, but his emotions were telling him different. Behemoths were complex creatures. They ruled their emotions tightly. When recording history, they tried to remove their emotions from the equation to ensure accuracy.

"We'll figure out who did this, Bernard. We were on our way to see Apollo. He probably has a clue to what is happening in all of this," I said trying to reassure him. It was hard though. I can't imagine how it would feel to watch your son slowly fade.

"Even if Apollo knows the answer, I won't hear it. The King has ordered us to move on with haste after his meeting with the Phoenix. I feel as if he wishes to leave this dark ordeal behind him, despite the fact that he will remember it always," Bernard replied. His words had a certain spite to them.

We sat in silence for a while until Bernard's ears perked up. "The King has returned." We all walked outside to meet him. Jeff had finally woken up and was giving the guards a hard time. The King looked much healthier than when I had last seen him. Both his head wounds had completely healed, I assume because of the Phoenix.

When the King noticed us outside waiting for him, he hurried his pace. "Quickly, the Phoenix has granted us double the feathers than we usually are given. Apply one to Benedict's forehead as quick as possible." Bernard complied and rushed to the tent. By the time I had gotten inside, the feather was already upon Benedict's head. Then right before our eyes Benedict's tusks began to regrow and his leg began to mend. He stood up and smiled at us all.

"What are you all looking at?" he said with in a semi shy tone. The feather began to glow and stayed on his forehead like it had been glued there. The King poked his head in to check on Benedict's progress and then his eyes got large in fear.

"Quickly, guards! Fetch water and rush it here," he called. He pushed in further into the tent, almost knocking it over. He seemed more worried than he did when he had two holes in his head.

"What is it?" I asked as I drew my sword. The feather continued to glow brighter and brighter. We all started to back up for fear of an explosive reaction.

"He is absorbing the magical properties of the feather! Since we are not magical creatures, this can have catastrophic consequences!" He exclaimed. Then the feather burst into flames upon Benedict's forehead. Within seconds the guards showed up and soaked Benedict.

Upon his forehead now rested a scar, already healed, in the shape of the feather. Then the King knelt on one leg and bowed to Benedict. "It is the mark of the Phoenix and the mark of our next king!" Bernard grew wide-eyed at hearing this and then knelt also. All of us, except for Jeff, joined in.

Bernard turned to us. "Only the King and his family have ever known how the next King of our race would be chosen. Who knew that our destiny was so deeply entwined with a highly magical being such as the Phoenix?"

The King let out a long cry of celebration and smiled. "Something good has finally come out of all this, then!" It was a happy moment for all of us, but in the back of my mind I was still thinking about Gunther.

When the uproar quieted down and everyone went back to their perspective task, I went to see the King. "King...or former King... or whatever. Are we able to use a Phoenix feather on Gunther, to heal him?"

The King let out a long sigh. "If I could, Danvel, I would. I relayed Gunther's situation to the Phoenix but was told that he must not come in contact with a feather. He has a highly magical wound and if any more magic than the sand that we put on his wound comes into contact with him, it may overwhelm him. That being said, I'm also saddened to ask you and your people to leave." The King had a weary look in his eyes but I didn't let that stop me from letting the rage build up in me.

"*What*? We just saved your asses and the asses of countless others!" I said raising my voice so everyone could hear. I once again drew my sword, pure anger radiating off of me. "If it weren't for me, you'd still have a damn sword in your head!"

"I understand all of these things, Danvel, but my people are wary of humanoids at the moment. They don't trust people who reek of the rains of Dragonia, especially. Plus, you have the sword with you. Please try and understand," the King pleaded. His voice was sincere but it did nothing to calm my rage.

"Oh, I understand alright. I understand how a bunch of scholars could be so closed minded to believe that all humanoids could be a threat to them." I sheathed my sword and smashed the ground with my fists, causing several tents to topple over. "Think about that next time you make me angry." I pointed at him, looking him straight in the eye so he knew I was serious. I wasn't afraid to take on the Behemoths.

I stormed off and went into the tent, Jeff had Gunther atop of him, still passed out, and Fox immediately merged with my sword. No words needed to be said. As we set off, Bernard and Benedict followed behind. "I thought you were leaving as soon as possible," I said, trying to temper my rage. I hadn't been this truly angry since I was a fledgling Dragon Slayer.

"Just following my King's orders to accompany you to the Dragon Slayer Temple. The new King that is," Bernard said with a grin. I tried to smile at this, but my anger was still present and Gunther still lay limp. Hopefully the rest of this journey would go fast.

Chapter 7 - Dragon Rage

Outside of the Dragon Slayer Temple

Midday

"It's more beautiful than I remember," Bernard commented. "Look at the Dragons on top of the pillars. When they built this temple, they put the Dragons there to remind the slayers that the Dragons are watching over us. On the Dragon Temple in the sky, there are humanoids etched into the bottom of the pillars to remind the Dragons that the world is built from and for them. The temple was put in the center of all the Patron Dragon Territories to represent the balance between everything. Balance between Light, Dark, Earth, Wind, Fire, and Water," He explained. Benedict listened intently while the rest of us listened intermittently.

I already knew most of what he was saying and Jeff had the attention span of a gnat. Gunther had woken up on two separate occasions on the way here. The first he was barely coherent and the second time he was able to stand up, eat, and then pass out again. I felt bad that he seemed to be getting the brunt of the hardships of our adventure, but it was fixing to end soon (hopefully), and perhaps Apollo could heal him the rest of the way.

Speaking of Apollo, he was waiting on the steps leading to the temple. "Hail, Apollo," I called out to him. Somehow I suspected he already knew we were coming. Despite being blind, Apollo always seemed to know things that were going on in the World within a day. It was almost as if the winds were talking to him. He had a grey beard that flowed down past his feet but somehow he never got tripped on it. It was like the beard had a mind to stay out of his feet's way.

"Hail, Danvel and company. Strange company that is. Two Behemoths, a Raiju, Jeff of course, and someone who has a bloodline unexpected. Strange company, indeed, Danvel." Everyone except Bernard and I were stunned. Not many knew who Apollo was, but those that did knew of his amazing powers. "Come in all! There is much to discuss."

We all followed Apollo into a massive hall where there were already seats to accommodate everyone, even the Behemoths. It was rumored that the temple opened into a pocket dimension and rooms would appear or disappear to satisfy whoever came into it. "Please make yourselves comfortable. I must speak with Danvel alone for a moment, however, then we shall all discuss what we need to discuss. Please do try and rouse Gunther while we are away." I followed Apollo out of the room and into a study like chamber with two chairs.

The study was marvelous, and one of a few of Apollo's studies that I hadn't seen yet. There were books strewn about on ancient history and old world magic. The walls had been adorned with different types of artifacts I assume are as old as the dirt we had just walked on.

"Where is the sword?" Apollo asked as soon as we sat down. The look of concern on his face made me know it was grave. I rarely saw Apollo wear a look so somber and have a demeanor so serious.

"It's in my supplies covered by cloth and tucked into a sheath. I haven't let anyone near it since I packed it away. Not even Jeff," I said, bringing my pack over. I pulled it out and as I started to remove the cloth, Apollo hissed.

"Keep it covered and let no one near it. It is the dark sword Muramasa. Forged by a dark soul of chaos. It has brought destruction throughout centuries and was thought to be lost when its dark powers sunk Atlantis." I wrapped the sword back up and hid it away. "Tell me, have you heard it talk to you at all?"

"No, nothing. No one else has mentioned anything at all," I replied giving him a curious look. I couldn't imagine a sword talking to me.

"Good," he replied. "The sword will speak to your mind and try to find a way to justify you releasing its dark power again. It preys upon self-doubt and dark thoughts. It has been the downfall of many good souls and has caused the deaths of millions, Danvel. It must never see the light of day. It is a true darkness from the ancient world."

"Well, you know that I got rid of my self-doubt in the Chamber of Mirrors. Nothing like facing every facet of yourself to help you get rid of that," I said trying to assure him. At least I didn't think I had any self-doubt.

"This is all good news. I have to ask you to take it with you when you leave though. Such darkness can't be left in a place like this. It would corrupt the magics in the place and turn the knowledge here towards dark purposes. It is the true manipulator. Be wary of it, Danvel." I had never seen Apollo this concerned before. It scared me to no end.

"You know I always heed what you have to say, Apollo. Your counsel is valued as if you were my father," I assured him. Apollo quickly changed his demeanor with a smile. He stood up and held his hand out to mine to help me out of the chair.

"Let us rejoin the others, then." We left the study and returned to the group who was chatting amongst themselves. Gunther was awake and munching on something from his pack, and looking much better than before. He had removed his bandage as well, revealing a fully healed arm. He was still pale, with dark bags under his eyes, but his overall manner seemed positive. It was a relief to know that he recovered so completely. Apparently that sand really was a miracle worker.

"First, it is a pleasure to meet you all," Apollo started. "I am the caretaker of the Dragon Slayer Temple and the Dragon Slayer legacy as well as many other minor things of no consequence. I helped train Danvel. I also maintain the great library of the continent Draco. There is none as comprehensive and hidden as it."

"You seem awfully bland to me," Gunther said with a guffaw. His lack of tact was astounding to even me. Apollo responded by throwing two kunai he had in his sleeve into the arm of the chair Gunther was sitting in. Gunther jumped up knocking himself and the chair onto the ground. He picked the chair up and tried to act inconspicuous.

"As you can see I am quite capable of handling myself. We have many matters to discuss so I would appreciate no more unwarranted interruptions." All eyes turned to Gunther who was trying to pry the kunai from his chair unsuccessfully and making a racket. "I would like to address our Behemoth guests first, if that is alright with everyone." Everyone nodded in agreement.

"A new king has arisen in the Behemoth ranks and that requires training. I would like to extend my services as a trainer to you. The world is changing faster than the Behemoth's old ways can keep up with at the moment and I feel a new type of King is needed. This breaks with a long line of tradition, but in light of recent events, I believe the Behemoths would benefit greatly. If it weren't for the out of the box thinking that you both displayed, many more would have died." Bernard looked as if he were about to say something but Apollo waved it off. "No answers yet, Bernard. Think over it for the day."

"Next, I would like to address Fox. Your family sends its regards and misses you every day. They send messages on the wind to you. If you wish I can show you how to send and receive them." For the first time in the adventure Fox seemed to show some emotion.

"I would like that very much, kind Apollo," Fox replied simply. The mention of his family made him almost seem remorseful for joining the trip. I felt guilty for bringing him along unnecessarily but if I hadn't we would have never saved the Behemoth King.

"Danvel and Jeff. While I am pleased to have you in my halls again, I am surprised that you are half the size," he said with a laugh. "You were supposed to get bigger with my training! Murlan is in the capital city of Wyrmvale, Heartha. He is outside the Dwarf Queen's castle and it seems he will be for a while. You should be able to reach him before he moves on."

I slammed my fist down on the side of the chair. "I hate Dwarves! They're all short and their beards are bigger than they are! They drink on the job! That's a safety hazard you know! Frickin Dwarves." Everyone looked at me as if I was strange.

"Irrational prejudices aside, Murlan is there. Now this brings me to the more serious part of the conversation." He let the air hang in anticipation and then turned to Gunther. "Gunther, I believe you to be the Dragon King's ancestor." This drew gasps from nearly everyone in the room. Bernard studied his features closely.

"I knew I thought he looked familiar before, but it was night most of the time we were in contact and it has been nearly one hundred and fifty years since I last spoke to the Dragon King. They are almost identical," Bernard said. "I met him when I was just a boy, like you Benedict. Seems like such a long time ago. I had just reached seventy and we spent a large amount of time in his castle looking through his library. I last saw him before the Dragon Council was disbanded and the Dragon Slayers replaced them." Apollo went to the next room and presented a painting of the King.

"He really does look like you, Gunther," I exclaimed as I slapped him on the shoulder. "Royalty around us this whole time! You... you're still going to be my squire, right?" Gunther gave me a smile then his face got serious for a moment. No one said anything as they waited for Gunther to react.

"Do you think that my parents were killed on purpose rather than by a Dragon suffering from Arcane Rot?" Gunther asked with a shocked look on his face. We all were saddened to hear his question. We both suffered great loss, but loss is even greater if there was a hidden purpose behind it all.

"Impossible to tell," Apollo commented. "Even for me. Something so far in the past and it happened in the blink of an eye. There also isn't a magical autopsy we can perform on a Dragon to tell if it was actually suffering from Arcane Rot or not. Magic is a tricky and swift thing. One moment it's there and the next it's left to a new host or to a pool of magic."

"I think I need to go take a walk," Gunther said, rising from his chair and leaving the room. I started to go after him but Apollo stopped me. Apollo was a master at seeing into someone's emotions and helping them understand themselves.

"I shall go after him. Better for no one to get lost in the temple today." And then Apollo was gone, leaving us by ourselves. We shuffled around silently, thinking about the revelations brought to us so suddenly.

"So what do you think of all this, Danvel?" Bernard asked, breaking the momentary silence. I stood up and paced a little bit before answering. It wasn't just that Gunther was royalty and whatever problems might crop up with that. It was that our journey could be coming to a close soon. The end was in sight.

"I think that Apollo is right about everything. He usually is. Benedict should train here and learn how to be a new type of king for the Behemoths. Apollo can teach you how to get information in new ways besides just traveling to library to library and hearing what you hear along the way. You'll be well versed in current events as well as history! Plus Apollo could totally teach you how to use his little pocket dimension trick. It's pretty awesome! What do you think, Benedict?"

Benedict excitedly launched himself off of his chair and proclaimed, "I want to stay and learn under Apollo! Think of all the ways we could help our people and other races. We could find ways to send cures to ailing villages and provide knowledges we have to anywhere we need!"

"And you won't be alone," I said with a keen smile. "Fox, I think you should stay here with Apollo as well."

Fox looked up at me in what I would guess was bewilderment. "But, sir. I wish to travel with you!" He sat up in his lounge chair and looked unsettled. He turned back into his wolf form suddenly. I imagine this was an automatic reaction when he became irritated.

"You might want to, but you want to hear from your family more. Stay with Apollo, learn what he wants to teach you and ask your family to come here. If someone is trying to cut off the Dragon Slayer Temple from the rest of the continent, then they might try something more bold coming up. I couldn't think of anyone else I'd trust with looking after Apollo than you." Fox was obviously moved by this. He then gave a smile. An electric wolf smile.

"Thank you, Danvel. For everything. First, you save my family from a terrible fate and now you bring us together again. Thank you so much." He was so jubilant that he transformed from a wolf into a cat. At least I assume that's why he changed. Magical creatures are strange. Also, I hate Dwarves.

"Do... do we still call you Fox? Because you're a cat now." Everyone in the room sort of tilted their heads to get a better view of Fox… cat...whatever.

"Fox will still suffice," Fox said with a chuckle.

"Then I suppose I just have to ask Jeff…," Jeff was asleep and by the amount of drool that was on the floor, he had most likely been asleep since Apollo and I had left the room. So I pushed him over into his own drool.

"N....nei... Neighhhh," Jeff said, smacking his lips as he woke up. "NEIGHHHH." Jeff leapt to his feet then slipped in his own drool and fell over. "Neighhhh," he said pathetically. This elicited laughter from everyone. Soon afterward Gunther and Apollo came in.

"Sorry for leaving, everyone," Gunther said somberly. He looked less upset than before, but he still didn't seem like the chipper person I was used to. "Apollo helped me sort it."

"No apology necessary, young Gunther," Bernard replied, speaking for all of us.

"I believe I forgot a piece of good news in all the previous talk," Apollo said. "I am in firm belief that the war between Dragonia and Wyrmvale will end very soon. My sources tell me that events are in motion that will bring an end to it. So let us celebrate! Follow me!" Apollo led us to great feast hall where a meal was already laid out for each of us.

"To the end of war! To the Dragon King!" I cried. Everyone raised their glasses and joined in the toast.

Chapter 8 - To the End of War

Outside of the Dragon Slayer Temple

Midday

"There is a secret path that leads between the Golem

Sanctuary and the Lakes of Astoria. It is about two miles southeast

and will lead you through a canyon. But be careful, it is said a giant

beast makes his home there. The passage hasn't been used in nearly twenty years," Apollo explained. "Now be on your way, Danvel. Return to your normal size." We said our goodbyes and were on our way.

Getting to the canyon proved easier than I hoped; either Apollo or some other force kept a path to it neatly maintained. There were various types of flowers, some I had never seen before, decorating the sides of the path. It was like a nexus of all the best parts of each country in Draco. The canyon, however, looked like it was the host to great battles between giants. Gashes in the canyon walls looked unnatural and the place reeked of death.

The canyon rose nearly a mile or so high, but only one hundred or so feet wide. Barely any sun was peeking through, making the canyon seem even more dismal. When we entered it, we found that there was almost a grey haze from all the dust and particulates in the air. The terrain was extremely uneven and we often found rockslides in our paths.

"Nice place Apollo sent us," I commented. Gunther shook his head in agreement.

"Do you ever get the feeling that he was only telling us half the truth?" Gunther asked. It was a question a lot of people seemed to have when they meet him.

"That's the way he does things. I don't know if it's a curse or what. I think he knows a lot of things he can't talk about. Probably has to do with the temple and all its secrets. He just directs us in a way so we don't get killed usually," I said with a half-smile. "Most of the time that is."

We continued down the canyon with no event for a few hours. We ran into several massive drops, which I assume were from waterfalls that existed long ago. They were difficult to traverse and even more difficult to get Jeff down along them. We ended up having to let him down first by tying him tightly with rope and slowing dropping him.

All of a sudden we began to hear the calls of many different birds. "Such a commotion," Gunther uttered under his breath.

"Neighhhhh," Jeff replied as he hunched down. He was more alert than I had seen him in a long time. More alert than when Bernard was stalking our camp in the desert.

"Get your bow out and ready, Gunther. Something is happening here. Jeff's on edge. He can understand the languages of other animals," I whispered. I pulled my sword and we creeped forward.

"HA HA HA HA, PUNY CREATURES," a voice called out from further down the canyon. We couldn't see anything from the haze and there was another steep drop off dead ahead. "Do you think you can sneak up to my lair and I not hear you?" A cyclops stepped out in to view. His head reached past the top of the canyon and he looked beastly. The canyon looked like it widened enough where he was just to allow him access inside it. "I am Prematorius, the greatest Cyclops on the continent and collector of…." he didn't get to finish his sentence before an arrow struck him in the eye and went through to his brain. He fell over dead.

"What the hell was that! You killed him mid-sentence!" I exclaimed. It was followed by a small coughing fit from everybody. The cyclops falling sent tons of dust our way and there was no escaping it.

"You told me to have my bow ready! I slipped! I can't help that the damn bow never misses!" Gunther explained. Jeff fell over laughing at this and I joined him. After our good laugh, we climbed over Prema whatever his name was and entered his lair, which was actually just a cave with curtains covering the entrance. Extremely cultured, this one.

We were surprised by what we saw. Birds, everywhere. And it smelled.... awful. "Didn't this guy know how to clean the bird cages? He must not have had a nose with that big eye!"

"Excuse me, please, can you help us?" a voice called out from the back of the cage.

"Ten Drakoins that there is a talking bird in the back of the cage," Gunther said. He pulled the coins out of his pack and gave them to Jeff.

"I'll take that bet," I replied, shaking his hand in agreement. What we found made the bet sort of hard to settle. A Harpy sat in the back of the cave, chained to the floor. "So is a Harpy a bird or a humanoid?" I whispered to Gunther. Gunther just shrugged. Her wings were extremely dirty and she looked like she had been chained there without any food for weeks.

"Please help us. The cyclops brokered for us from the far corners of the world. He's crazy!" She started crying, hard. It was sad to see the state that some of these birds and birdlike creatures were in.

"Excuse me; the correct term is he WAS crazy. He's dead. Slain by the mighty Gunther," I said, lifting Gunther's arms in the air like a champion. Jeff aided with a dance. After a few moments of celebration, I pulled my sword out and destroyed her shackle.

Gunther and Jeff went to work opening up the bird cages and setting loose the birds as I helped the Harpy to the cave entrance and gave her directions to the Dragon Slayer Temple. "Now, don't act like a Harpy usually does and I'm sure that Apollo won't kill you right away," I said with a slight bit of sarcasm. Apollo didn't have a fondness for hybrid creatures. He also didn't like killing. So it was about a fifty-fifty chance that he'd help.

"Mr. Danvel, quickly come here," Gunther called from further in the cave. I hustled over leaving the Harpy to save herself. Gunther was standing over a cage housing a Finch.

"What's up, Gunther." The cage was open but the bird remained in it, hopping around.

"Either I'm starting to understand the birds or the bird wants to thank us for helping it escape."

"Indeed it is the latter. The Language of the Birds is highly complex and not for the faint of heart. However, the human language is far easier to understand. I am Jenico and I am now in your debt. In my cage is a whistle. Use it at any time and I will come to your aid. There are far too few good citizens nowadays. Thank you for your help." Then Jenico flew away. I reached in the cage… it was disgusting, and pulled out the whistle. I handed it to Gunther.

"You're the one who slayed the cyclops. It is totally your whistle." Gunther grabbed the whistle and shoved it in his pack making sure not to touch any of his food. We double checked the cave and went on our way. "Cyclopses are weird."

The rest of the canyon was uneventful and bland. The sun barely shone through at times and the air continued to reek of various different smells, none of them good. The fresh air from Wyrmvale, however, was a fantastic reprieve. "Just wait till you see the countryside of Wyrmvale, puts Dragonia's to shame."

We broke free of the canyon and breathed in deeply. The countryside was immaculate. Farms off in the distance, blue skies, and green, dry grass. Gunther and Jeff were enjoying it too. Gunther was lying down in the fresh grass and Jeff was smelling some nearby flowers. It was a good moment after a string of bad moments for us. I took it all in; trying to make sure I remembered this moment in our adventure.

That and the possibility of the end of the war... Getting changed back to our normal size...Things were looking up. "Let's get going, Wyrmvale isn't a small country." It wasn't that Wyrmvale was bigger than the other countries on the continent Draco (they were all roughly the same size), it was the fact that Wyrmvale consisted of mostly rolling hills, valleys, forested mountains. All very beautiful but took more of a toll to traverse than the flatlands of Dragonia. It was also easier to get lost since there wasn't a lake with a distinct shape to guide you.

We walked nearly all day before we saw any new signs of civilization. A small farm on the edge of a lake. We got closer when we realized how small of a farm it was.... a Gnome farm. The only place that we could have fit was the barn and only one of us would have fit at that so we continued on our way.

"I forgot that a large amount of the farming in Wyrmvale was done by Gnomes," I said as Jeff and Gunther drug their feet behind me.

"I've never seen a Gnome before," Gunther said groggily.

"Neigh," Jeff said.

"Jeff's right; you aren't missing much. They're basically small humans who wear pointy hats. Did you notice that even his front door had a point on it so his hat could make it through? Legend has it that if you see a Gnome without his hat then you have three days to make your peace with life and then you die. Weird creatures them Gnomes."

"Can we make camp?" Gunther droned. We were near a forest, which in my experience is never good, but we also weren't going to make it anywhere tonight so I agreed. The forest stretched for miles and there was no getting around it for the day. Jeff collected firewood while Gunther and I set up makeshift tents and got our food ready. It was the first true camp that we were able to construct on our adventure. No rain, no sand, no danger. It felt good.

After everything was settled and we ate, Gunther was pushing for stories of the past. "C'mon Mr. Danvel. I'm sure you have some stories to tell. Tell me about one of your adventures!" I gave out a great sigh in reply.

"First, why don't you tell me how your adventure right now is going, Gunther? Are you discovering yourself? Or is it getting foggier?" Gunther spent the next few minutes in silence, kicking at the fire every now and then. It was the first time I felt Gunther was really thinking everything that has happened over. Even though we had only been on this adventure for a relatively short time, a potential lifetime of events had already happened for some people. "I think... I think I'm learning a lot about myself. I want on this quest to find out who I was, and you know I think I really found out. I'm royalty, despite that it basically means nothing unless the Dragons and the humanoid rulers recognize me. I'm definitely clumsy. I act without thinking a lot of the time. I think that's just you rubbing off on me. Except it always seems to end up working out better for you." I gave out a small laugh and Jeff whinnied slightly in response.

"I just have better luck than you is all. Actually, it's all a matter of keeping a cool head. Sure I get angry a lot, but I try not to let it cloud my assessment of the current situation. That comes with time and experience."

"What about you, Mr. Danvel, Jeff? Have you found yourself?" I smiled at this question.

"I think doing all that I've done; I'm still the same man I was. I shouldn't have really doubted it, but with the Dragon laughing at me and the way Gale acted… It was hard to believe I was the same man."

"Neighhhhhhhh," Jeff said.

"Jeff feels the same way. We're a team now. It makes all of this easier."

"Now, let's hear a story, Mr. Danvel. Since we all know who we are, let's hear about who you were."

"Alright, this is one before Jeff and I met. When you're born into the Dragon Slaying life, it's more than just being born that way. You have to undergo trials to activate the latent magic inside you. Apollo hadn't trained a Dragon Slayer since before my grandfather (yes he's that old) and he wasn't sure if the old ways would suffice, especially since I have all of the Dragon Slayer magic in me. Before it used to be spread out among fifteen to twenty, even forty once, Dragon Slayers at a time."

By the time I had gotten this far in the story, Jeff was asleep but Gunther was avidly interested. "So instead of the usual two trials that a usual Dragon Slayer had to face, Apollo assigned me five. The Water Roulette, the Fire Dance, the Earth Catacombs, the Wind Chasms, and finally the Chamber of Mirrors. They were meant to fortify my mind, body, and spirit and make me travel all across Draco and learn about the world."

"The Water Roulette was probably the second hardest trial since I had no idea what to expect from the trials. Plus its name implied I had a chance to die regardless of what I did. The first part of each trial was finding out where they existed, so I spent weeks in the libraries of Dragonia trying to discover its location. That was when I found the book that explained everything. It was called…. 'The Location of All the Dragon Slayer Trials.' It cost me two Drakoins. Apparently Apollo had written it years ago and either forgotten it or just didn't tell me."

"So I get a small boat and row my way out to the said location and… nothing. I waited for a half day until something happened. What I had skimmed over in the book was that these events only happen at a certain time each day and this was when the sun was setting. So here we go with the sun setting and the sea looking like it's on fire, and then the whirlpools appear. Six of them. So we have these six fire whirlpools and I have to choose one. Not only do I have to choose one, but if I don't choose one by the time the sun sets, they all merge and I die. Not only that, but no one knows where these lead because anyone who chooses the wrong one was never seen."

"So I picked one and jumped down. The current had me for a while but eventually I was led down to a cave with a chest inside of it. Inside the chest was this necklace." I pulled it from my neck and gave it to Gunther. The necklace houses a small crystal in it that had an amber glow. "Apollo told me that the crystal houses the magic of a legendary dragon that gave itself up to give life to the Dragon Slayer Order. He believed that the Dragons were gaining too much power so there needed to be someone to check it."

"After I got the necklace, the book told me the trial was over, but I wasn't satisfied. So I went back the next day facing the same direction and jumped into a different whirlpool. I continued until I jumped into them all. Each whirlpool led to a different chest that had a different necklace, each containing Dragon essences of each element."

"I thought there were only four Dragon elements. Do you carry each necklace? What do they all mean?" Gunther said, fascinated. Apparently the scholar in him was coming out, or perhaps learning that he was royalty had caused him to be more curious about the Dragons.

"There are only four elements that most people know about. The other two are hidden apparently. I'm just telling you what Apollo told me. As far as the location of each necklace. Only the people who carry them know where they are. I split them up to be safe in case something were ever to happen to me. As far as what they all mean? Who the heck knows? Could be something big, could be something insignificant."

"Now back to the trials. The second trial was actually pretty easy. The Fire Dance was to trek across the Volcano Valley. Like the previous trial, time was a big factor. The valley was usually filled with lava but for twenty minutes a day, it was clear. So I had to run across the hot valley, collect the stone and run back. The stone rested in a tree that was rooted in the cliff wall. The problem was that the stone was stuck in the tree. So I ripped the tree off the wall and ran. I barely made it lugging the thing but overall, pretty easy."

"What was the stone?" Gunther inquired.

"It was another Dragon crystal. All of the trials collected them. So after getting that stone and a week's worth of resting my semi burnt feet, I moved on to the third trial. The Earth Catacombs are where they bury the great Earthwyrms of the realm. I was already uneasy in this trial because of my predisposed hatred towards Earthwyrms. I hadn't let go of it yet and part of me was still seeking vengeance."

"The place was pretty creepy. A lot of pent of magic from all of the Dragons. The stone was in the grave of one that was long deceased. It was more of a test of will that I could do it rather than some arduous task that tested my abilities. I didn't sleep for a week after that. It isn't easy to dig up someone's remains."

From behind us the leaves began to rustle and spooky noises began to ring out from the forest. Gunther scrambled for his bow as the sounds got closer. Before he could get a handle on his bow, Jeff pounced out on top of him. I lost it as Gunther screamed and freaked out. Eventually, he regained his composure and pushed Jeff over.

Jeff replied by mimicking Gunther when he was freaking out. He then returned to his sleeping as Gunther scowled.

"Can I finish the story you requested, or do I need to wait for you to enact revenge on Jeff?" I asked, growing impatient. Stories aren't for interrupting.

"Please do, Mr. Danvel," Gunther replied. I got myself back into story telling mode and continued.

"After I finally settled down from the previous trial, I traveled to the north. Not many people go to Drakeland due to its unpredictable weather and the fact that the Drakes and Yetis are generally inhospitable. And by generally I mean most people go their whole lives without seeing a Wind Drake and a Yeti. The Wind Chasms were exactly like what they sounded. A bunch of massive chasms that one could only get past if they rode the winds."

"At the end of the Chasms sat a nest that was said to be the source of all the winds, but from the beginning of the trial you could tell that there wasn't anything in the nest, at least that was what I thought. The first time I jumped I barely made it to the other side. I didn't time it right with the wind and it ended a few seconds before I needed it to. Two more tries and one almost near death experience where I had to climb up a fairly long distance and I had mastered the timing. Finally, I had reached the nest and found that the wind was really coming from the it! Inside there was a miniaturized Wind Dragon."

"A miniature? Like you?" Gunther said with a roaring laughter. I hit him. Gunther tumbled back into Jeff who woke up and responded by head-butting him. Gunther stood up groggily and plopped back down. "What I meant to say is that you are looking magnificently violent at the moment."

"I believe that is the correct answer. The Wind Drake told me that he had been there since the start of the trials and hadn't seen one of me for a while. He gave me the last crystal and I was on my way. When I returned to Apollo with the crystals he told me that these crystals unlocked the Chamber of Mirrors. Usually a Dragon Slayer would only have one or two of these crystals but since I had collected all nine of them, the experience would be more intense."

I took a drink from my flask and continued. "The Chamber of Mirrors is actually in the lower levels of the Dragon Slayer Temple, only accessible if Apollo allows it. So he led me down there and we put the crystals in the door and I went in. The chamber housed nine mirrors; I assume one for each of the crystals. Then nine versions of me stepped out of the mirror. I had to deal with them one by one until they were gone. Only then I could leave."

Gunther took a sip from his cup. "What do you mean versions of you?"

"One of me where my anger from when my parents had died had taken over me. My doubts. My fears. Everything that makes me who I am was there. Good and bad. That's why I'm often so sure of myself. I've had to face my self-doubt looking right at me and overcome it. When I emerged, my magic was activated and I got all my Dragon Slayer strength."

"So if the crystals exist for the Dragon Slayer Trials, why do you have one around your neck?" Gunther asked, still completely enthralled by the tale.

"Once I told you we all have our burdens to bear. I'm the last of the Dragon Slayer line. Dragon Slayers generally don't find someone to love and settle down with. They usually die in some horrific way by a crazed dragon. So we gave the crystal to people we trust in case they're ever needed. Needed for what, I don't know."

"Wow, I almost wish I had a tale like that. I guess getting to live them through people works too, though." Gunther let out a long yawn.

"Almost is right," I said with a chuckle. "If you had gone through them you'd almost wish you hadn't. Now get to bed, I'll take first watch. Jeff will be up when it's his turn." Gunther obliged and went into his makeshift tent, leaving me alone. I put my necklace back on and got my pack out. I reached inside and pulled out a small box. Inside the box was a ring with the same magic crystal attached to it. "Oh, Gale. Soon I'll be back to normal and maybe I won't have to bear this burden alone," I said quietly to myself. I spent the rest of my watch with it in my hand and my eyes on the forest.

Chapter 9 - Look to the Sky

Wyrmvale

Edge of Some Forest

Morning

The morning started just like any other. Us arguing about which direction was the right direction. "No, we just came from that way!" I yelled, gesturing at the direction Gunther was sure that we were supposed to go. How he figured that he knew better than I did, I don't know. I'm the only one that has actually been in Wyrmvale before.

"Just because you are the only one of us who has been here doesn't mean you just know everything! We need to go that way!" Gunther yelled back.

"Neighhhhh, "Jeff said. Trying to point out that he thought the going through the forest was the best choice.

"There's only one way to settle this," I said. "Sword, Shield, Claw!"

Jeff spun around in a circle in excitement as Gunther looked confused. "What the heck is that, Mr. Danvel?"

"It's a deciding game. Sword beats Claw, but is beaten by Shield. Shield beats Sword, but loses to Claw. Claw beats Shield, but loses to Sword. Whoever wins the game gets to choose where we go. You and me first Gunther!" I showed him the symbols for each one. A finger for sword, an open palm for shield and three fingers for claw.

I pumped my fist three times and opened up with Sword. Gunther didn't pump with me and opened later than I did. "What the hell was that? You have to do it at the same time as me or you're cheating!" We tried fifteen more times before Gunther got it right.

Gunther chose Claw and I chose Sword. "LOSERRRRRR," I yelled while doing a small victory dance. I pushed Gunther over and did the dance again.

"Neighhh," Jeff said loudly. Jeff was the undefeated champion in Sword Shield Claw. Somehow he always knew what I was going to pick.

"Let's do this!" Jeff and I pumped three times. I picked Claw but Jeff somehow knew it and picked Shield. "DANG IT! EVERY TIME JEFF, EVERY TIME!" Gunther stared at me in bewilderment as I raged around the edge of the forest.

"Mr. Danvel... you do know that Jeff can only pick Shield, right? He doesn't have any fingers."

"He'd like you to think that, Gunther. But he's a brilliant mastermind. And now we're going into the forest which is probably infested with... things! Because he's EVIL!" Jeff replied by sticking his tongue out at me.

"Excuse me, I couldn't but help overhearing," a soft voice said from inside the forest. I pulled my sword and pointed it at the source of my voice. A massive tree began moving, only to reveal that it was not a tree, but a Tree Dragon. "Whoa, human. No need to act drastically. I was just hoping to point you in the right direction. Where is it you seek?"

Tree Dragons are typically the easiest going Dragons of them all, but are rarely sighted because of their fantastic camouflage. They housed a tree on their neck and many believe that the tree roots are actually part of the Dragon's spine. This particular Dragon had a massive Cedar Tree on its back. The tree rose nearly fifty feet in the air, making the Dragon seem like it would have trouble walking, but it bore it well. It seemed extremely mobile, which made me more wary.

"Who's asking?" I replied, still keeping my sword on him. I immediately ran my eyes over the camp to make sure that nothing was missing. "Gunther! Check our packs, make sure everything is there."

"I am Cedarn, of the Cedar Woods. I truly am only trying to help. Where do you plan on going to?" he said giving us a smile, which revealed wooden teeth.

"Everything's here, Mr. Danvel." I lowered my sword but still kept it in my hand.

"Out of the three of you, you all picked the wrong direction," he said laughing a mighty, wooden, laugh. "Come, pack up your things and I shall take you. It is barely a day's walk." We began packing up our things and when I got to my pack I noticed that the cloth around Muramasa had come undone slightly. Maybe I had knocked it when I was putting the ring back into its place. I'm sure that's what it was.

Cedarn kept a moderate pace with us. Tree Dragons have tremendous gaits and can often outpace any other Dragon, well, ones that don't have massive trees on their back like this one. He was still incredibly limber. Their treelike appearance often misleads adventurers into thinking that they are incredibly slow creatures.

We made small talk as we walked and I recounted the tale of what brought us all here to Wyrmvale. To our surprise and relief, Cedarn had no problem that we were from Dragonia. In fact, he said that the citizens of Wyrmvale usually went out of their way to make Dragonians feel welcome despite the war.

This made us feel slightly uncomfortable since Leviathan and Baron Dexter had set out a law that tried to prohibit Wyrmvalians from passing through Dragonia. I heard tales of how they were cast out from Dragonia to Drakeland with no supplies to battle the cold or hunger. I didn't approve of how it was conducted but Dragon Slayers don't get a say on the laws.

Cedarn also gave us some intriguing information. All trade from Drakeland had been cut off. They believed that perhaps Leviathan and Tiamat were in discussion to bring an end to the war and didn't want any traders to be seen as spies in the meeting. This made us excited since it all but confirmed Apollo's word.

True to Cedarn's word, we made it to Heartha before dark settled in. Although it would've probably been better if it was dark so I didn't have to see so many damn Dwarves! Dwarves everywhere! Working and drinking, singing and drinking, drinking and drinking. "Where to the nearest inn?" I asked with gritted teeth and clenched fists.

Cedar pointed to the edge of town. "The Pink Oak Inn is over there. Have a safe adventure, little one," I thanked him hurriedly and rushed to the inn, booking us a room and holing up in it. Jeff and Gunther walked in soon after.

"What the hell was that?" Gunther asked. "Did you think you were going to attack the whole Dwarf populace or something?" Gunther and Jeff began to laugh.

"You say it like it's a joke! I just didn't prepare myself for all of the Dwarves. I didn't think I'd want to fight them all so soon." Gunther and Jeff laughed even harder. "It's not funny! I just want to punch them all!" They continued laughing as they unpacked their gear.

"We're going to go travel the town and look for Murlan. Are you going to come with?"

"I think I should go to a pub and get information there. If I get in a bar fight then it won't be a big deal," I replied nervously. "And I'll find that damn guy for Galen," I said as I pulled the stone from my pack, still in the cloth.

"Why do you think he said not to touch it to lead?" Gunther grabbed the stone from me and opened the cloth. "It doesn't look like much."

I swiped the stone back and raised it the lantern in the room. "No it doesn't. But unless we have something lead, we won't know."

Gunther grabbed his pack excitedly, saying, "Wait a second!" He then pulled like ten things from his pack, all of them lead.

"You've been carrying lead things in your pack this whole time?" I slapped him on the arm. "What the hell? That must have made the journey twice as hard!"

"I guess it's good training, then. Let's try it." I complied and touched the stone to the lead objects. Right before our eyes, they turned to gold.

"Holy moly," Gunther exclaimed. "We are so keeping this!" I slapped Gunther upside the head, something that felt more and more uplifting every time I did it.

"No, we aren't! We made a promise to Galen and we're keeping it. Plus, I owe him a TON of money. Let's get going. I want to find Murlan before it's totally dark out."

It didn't take long to find a pub. Apparently there were at least fifteen in Heartha. Much to my chagrin, it was packed with Dwarves. I swallowed my righteous anger and went to the bar. "Give me your best mead, barkeep! And some information on the side!"

The barkeep took me in then pushed over a mug and leaned in close. He reeked of mead and smoke. He was an older Dwarf. Had to be over eighty by the amount of greys in his beard.

Dwarves aged slower than most humanoids and only showed it in their beards. The amount of greys signaled how old they are. Male Dwarves were proud of their graves while the females hated the acknowledgement of it.

"What kind of information you looking for, slayer?" he said with a keen grin. It was obvious he was well informed and lucrative because of it. I pushed him ten Drakoins.

"I'm looking for Murlan. I heard that he's set up near here but I need an exact location. I'm also looking for a broker of legendary weapons," I said slyly, trying to look inconspicuous.

"Murlan? That insufferable wizard? I would've paid you to take care of him. Although with what he's done with you, I bet you'd do it for free. He's in a huge tent at the other side of town. You'll be able tell it's his by the fact that it looks like a wizard's hat. He's kind of a jerk."

"As for the broker? The one you're looking for is about three buildings down from here. Guy's a word we Dwarves don't say in pubs." Pubs were the Dwarves holy places.

The barkeep pushed my Drakoins back at me. "We don't take money from slayers. You guys help keep the world safe. Not a fee to be gained from that but you do it anyways."

It felt nice to be recognized, even though I still disliked the notion of being complimented by a Dwarf. I downed my mead and thanked him. It was good mead and gave me a buzz instantly. No wonder the Dwarves drink it all the time. Heck, I didn't even feel all that angry at the Dwarves anymore when I looked at them. Good mead. The barkeep handed me another one.

"To the Dragon Slayer!" he cried. "Da fug!" Da fug was an ancient Dwarven saying calling for everyone in the bar to chug their mead. We all chugged our mead and I left the pub a celebrity. Why did I hate Dwarves again? Mostly the singing.

I followed the barkeep's directions and found the place that Galen needed me to drop the stone off at. When I walked in, the setup looked exactly like Galen's store. Fake merchandise everywhere. I rang the doorbell and was stunned by what I saw. The guy walking out of the building looked exactly like Galen.

"What are you staring at? I don't have all day to wait on you," he barked impatiently. Just like Galen would have.

"Are you a twin to Galen in Dragonia?" I asked still stunned at the similarities.

"What the hell are you talking about, kid? I barely know the guy. Just know he owes me lots of money and what not. Are you his delivery service or something?" I didn't like his tone, but like Galen, he was probably wearing some sort of armor that protected him so I decided not to push it. We walked in and I slammed the stone down on the counter.

"Or something. Is that what you're looking for?" He very excitedly grabbed the stone from the counter.

"I'll be right back, kid," he said rushing out of the room. In short time he was back. "Tell Galen we're even. Now get out of here!" I thought about burning his store down as I left, but the pub was only three buildings down, and I didn't want to accidentally set it alight as well.

I, then, went to the other side of town and found the tent exactly where the barkeep said it would be. He was right. Murlan was a jerk. The tent stood taller than every other building around it except for the Dwarf Castle. Decorated a brighter color than all the other buildings and the stars on the tent shone different hues.

The Dwarf Castle was massive and put Leviathan Castle to shame. It was beautiful in its design and function. Turrets made the castle look unique, but also housed several automatic weapons in case of siege. It shone a brilliant green, the color of James, the Patron Dragon, a feat that I have no idea how they accomplished. There were rumors that the castle actually extended further underground than it stood in the air. Dwarves love to work and live underground (most Dwarves slept in the "basements" of their houses). The top of the castle was generally considered to be a meeting ground for emissaries and council meetings. As I was about to enter, Jeff and Gunther showed up.

"You beat us," Gunther said, stunned. "We walked around the whole town to find it! What the heck?"

"And I had some mead and got treated as a hero! That's two wins in one! Now, who is ready to meet this pathetic wizard?" We all walked in to find a mess everywhere. Books thrown about, scrolls open and undone, food half uneaten and left. It looked like that time Jeff agreed to house sit for my now ex-girlfriend.

I walked over to one meal and took a deep sniff. "This is still fresh, so he must be here. Also, he undercooks his food," I said after I took a bite. MURLAN!!! MURLANNNNNN!!!!!" I continued to shout as we walked through his place. The further we went in, the more of a mess it was.

As we neared the back, I began to hear mumbling. "Alakazam… no that's stupid… it can't be right," the voice said. "Claatu? No that's even worse." As we rounded the corner, there Murlan sat reading a particularly lengthy scroll. Murlan was taller than most humans (maybe magic did that). He had a lengthy black beard and looked like he hadn't slept for weeks. His clothes didn't match and his once large wizard hat was a child's size.

"Murlan! What the hell is your problem?" I called as I stormed over in front of him. His beard housed several crumbs and things I didn't want to think about what they were. He was obviously a slob or oblivious to everything.

"I'll be with you in a minute, Danvel," he said, dismissing me. Then he looked up in shock. "Oh my gosh! It is you ,Danvel! And you're alive! And you're small just like everything else!" He came over and gave me an unexpected hug, lifting me in the air, until I slapped him upside the head.

"What the hell did you do to me?" I screamed. "I'm freaking miniature! And then you left me!" I slapped him again.

"I can explain it. I can explain it. I can explain it! I think. I believe that I was cursed. When I cast the spell it was the first one I had cast since Wyrmvale. And when you turned small and rushed off I didn't have time to go after you. I figured that I had just killed the last Dragon Slayer. So I packed up and ran. Everything else I tried to cast spells on came with the same result. Tiny and or cute. Look at my damn hat!"

"So who cursed you?" Gunther asked, butting in.

Murlan let out a long sigh. "I believe it was the Dwarf Queen, Storm. Dwarves hate wizards and I may... have... incidentally insulted her beard."

"Why would you do that?" Gunther and I shouted at the same time. "You see? Even Gunther knows that's a bad idea. What did you say to her?"

"I told her the grey hairs in her beard looked majestic. It did not go over well. They threw me out right away. Ever since I found out I've been trying to reverse it myself and get an audience with the Queen. Nothing has worked, however. No reversal, no audience."

"Well that's because you haven't had a Dragon Slayer with you. The Dwarves consider me a hero. We're going to go tomorrow," I said as I flexed.

"But, I," Murlan started.

"But, nothing. And you better not run off this time. We'll be in the Pine Oak Inn." We left and returned to the inn. Tomorrow was going to be a big day.

Chapter 10 - A Dragon of a Time

Wyrmvale

Outside The Dwarf Castle

Morning

"I formally request an audience with the Queen," I announced in front of the castle gate. Murlan stood beside me and Jeff and Gunther behind me.

"Who is it that requests an audience with her?" the Dwarf at the gate responded. Normally I'd have wanted to pummel him but three glasses of mead helped a lot. I had stopped into the pub, which was packed with the exact same amount of Dwarves as the night before… except it was morning.

"I am Danvel the Dragon Slayer and this is my party. We come from the Dragon Slayer Temple after a long journey."

"A Dragon Slayer? You may have an audience, but only one member of your party may accompany. You may also carry no weapons. Hurry along." I gave my sword and pack to Gunther. The Dwarf guard was lucky that I was giving my weapons or I'd teach him a lesson about telling a Dragon Slayer to hurry along. Murlan gave Jeff his staff and we headed in after the Dwarf.

The inside of the Dwarf Castle was as magnificent as the outside. Their training yard was lush and magnificent, utilizing different types of plants as training mechanisms. Earthwyrms seemed to work perfectly in sync with the Dwarves. Compared to Dragonia, this seemed like an utopia.

On the other side of the castle there were tunnels leading underneath, I assume to the ore mines and their blacksmiths. What many people didn't know was that underground Wyrmvale was as rich in ores as the topside was in plant life.

He led us through halls that were decorated in magnificent colors and treasures. Ores shaped into great tools and weapons. Mirrors with magical properties. Statues of the Dwarf royalty. It was truly a wondrous castle and the throne room didn't disappoint. The throne was decorated with gold, silver, and other wondrously colored ores I hadn't seen before.

The Dwarf Queen sat on her throne looking mighty. She was wearing a dark green dress with gold trimmings. Her crown, while small, housed several large jewels. She had a ring on each of her fingers, each a different color from the Wyrmvale banner.

Each country had a humanoid liaison to power. Wyrmvale had the Dwarf Queen, Dragonia had a human Baron, Salamandra had a King of the Lion Pride, and Drakeland had the Yeti Lord. They served as direct "rulers" to the humanoid populace and liaison between the humanoids and the true power, the patron Dragon.

Murlan bowed as was custom in these gatherings. I did not bow. I bow to no Dwarf! The Queen took no notice at me and began cursing as soon as she saw Murlan. "Who allowed this daft piece of no good wizard into my castle? He is a disgrace!" To Murlan's credit, he didn't budge at the insults, if anything he just bowed deeper.

"I don't disagree with any of those points," I said happily. "I am Danvel, the Dragon Slayer. I have brought Murlan here today with me because we have a request of you." I tried to speak as straight and true as possible. Dwarves, especially their queen, didn't appreciate double talk or fancy ways of saying things.

"A request? Pfft, of course that is what you want. A wizard who insults me then has a request." She stood up and stomped her feet. She began pacing angrily.

"It actually more has to deal with me. See, we believe that you cursed Murlan after he intelligently insulted your beard," I said placing an immense amount of sarcasm on the intelligently part.

"Which I am totally sorry for," Murlan spoke up, still bowing.

"SHUT UP!" Both the Queen and I yelled. We smiled at each other. She wasn't half bad for a Dwarf.

"I did indeed curse you, Murlan. It was only fitting that someone who insulted the great Dwarf Queen be cursed to make things look dwarf like in size. Something to always remind you of the disservice you brought to us. Now, how is this relevant, Danvel?"

"You see, Murlan cast his spell on my Sleipnir and me causing us to shrink in size. While I agree this is an apt curse for Murlan to live with, I wish to be restored to my own size. Jeff would like it as well. So could you like… uncurse us?" I asked pleading. As much as I was getting used to being wee, I wanted to be normal again.

The Queen returned to her throne and lounged in it as she thought over my request. Murlan remained bowing the whole entire time. "Very well. Guards, please fetch me my amulet." She made a dismissive hand gesture and then they were gone. We spent the next few moments in silence. What does one say to a stuck up Queen? I passed the time by leaning on Murlan.

Shortly after the guards had left, they returned with a shining amulet. A bright diamond sat in the middle of a white gold enclosure. It was the largest diamond I had ever seen. It had a glow of magic about it. "This will only take a few moments," she said as she walked over to a stain-glassed window. She opened the curtains to let the light in, which all seemed to get caught in the amulet as she held it up.

She began to chant some words and then the sunlight was gone. Replaced by an odd looking shadow. A Dragon shadow. There was a large commotion outside and then a crash. Then the Dragon shadow became a Dragon. The Queen retreated as a Wind Drake crashed through the castle wall, snarling.

Drakes were usually smaller than the average Dragons, but had the ability to fly. Their wingspan was nearly twice the length of their whole bodies. Their scales looked like feathers and were supposed to function as such, but no one ever really studied them up close. Their smallness didn't make them any less intimidating or ferocious, however.

"What is the meaning of this?" she cried, grabbing for a sword. The Dragon was on her in seconds, ignoring her question. I jumped over and struck the Dragon twice, causing it to retreat. The guards rushed over to the Queen and Murlan joined me at the window.

Wind Drakes, close to one hundred, were all over the town, wreaking havoc. Dwarves were rushing out of their houses and the pub armed with pickaxes and swords. Some of them were met with grisly fates as Drakes were waiting to meet them. Houses were set ablaze and families trapped inside.

"The Queen is dead," the guards said as they came up behind us. I looked back and saw that the amulet was crushed. I felt a moment of despair for myself and Jeff but swallowed it quickly. These people needed me now. They needed a Dragon Slayer.

"By God. A Dragon war has started. A real Dragon war. We are in no way ready for this," I said in awe. "Murlan, go downstairs and find Jeff and Gunther. Tell Gunther that he shouldn't hold back with the arrows. Guards. Arm everyone and start getting people into the castle."

"What are you going to do?" Murlan asked, starting towards the door.

"I'm taking a shortcut," I replied. I jumped out of the window and landed on the nearest Wind Drake. The Drakes had no riders (Yetis were rumored to ride the Drakes to decrease travel times) which was even more curious. I struck down hard at the Drake I was on, causing it to veer towards the ground. I gave it another good smack and it went unconscious; they were apparently not as sturdy as the other Dragons. In typical Dragon Slayer fashion I landed right in front of Jeff and Gunther arriving right before Murlan.

"That's twice I've beaten everyone in the race to our destination," I said as I landed. Gunther and Jeff looked confused as Murlan scooped up his staff from the ground.

"You said you were taking a shortcut!" Murlan yelled.

"Sword please," I called to Gunther, holding my hand out. "Murlan, I beat you. Start moving faster." Gunther placed my sword in my hand. I returned to the unconscious Dragon and disposed of it. "No mercy right now. We have to save as many people as we can so that means killing. Anyone have a problem?" They all shook their heads, no.

"Jeff, you're on rescue duty. No complaints. You're useless in the air and you know it. Gunther, start shooting those arrows. You know you can't miss. Dwarf," I said pointing to the nearest one, "get as many arrows as you can for this young man."

"What do you want me to do?" Murlan asked.

"You make those bastards tiny and cute! Most of them won't realize that they have the same strength and they'll have trouble adjusting to their weight and new wing span," I barked at him.

"Where are you going then," he asked as he put on his miniature hat.

"I'm going to learn how to fly," I said with a smile. I rushed into the castle and found the armory. Inside was what I wanted, a catapult that was big enough to launch a rock the length of a city. I pushed it through the crowds, out of the castle, and into the streets. There was a Dwarf nearby finishing off a Wind Drake and I motioned him over. "Send me flying," I said heroically.

The Dwarf looked at me astonished. "You're insane. Those Dragons will tear you apart, and if you miss the fall will kill you." I jumped inside of it anyways.

"I better not miss then!" He sighed and cut the rope sending me flying in the sky. From the sky I got a crystal clear point of view of the battle. The Dwarves were losing badly. Despite the superior numbers and advanced weaponry, the Dwarves were ground oriented creatures and had a complete disadvantage against the Wind Drakes. After looking at all of this I remembered I was still in the air.

It wasn't the worst feeling of terror I've ever had, though. The worst came when the arc started to take me downward and I still hadn't found a Dragon to hitch a ride on. Despite having huge wings I couldn't find one that was willing to stay in place. Just as I was about to crash into a house, I landed on the Dragon that was flying about to light it on fire.

"Thanks for the soft landing." I said as I separated his head from his body. I launched myself off of him and onto another, repeating what I had done. There were Dragons dropping all around me, either from my sword, Gunther's arrows, or Murlan's body changing magic. That's when I looked beyond Heartha and saw the reinforcements coming. Nearly triple the size as the original attack force. I descended safely using the Dragon I had just disposed of.

"JEFFF," I yelled over the commotion. Jeff came running, tackling a Dragon that just landed and slammed it into a building. I joined the fray and stopped the Dragon. "Jeff, how is the evacuation going," I asked as I helped him out of the broken building.

"Neighhh," Jeff replied, despondent.

"Well good job at least getting the south of town evacuated to the castle. I think the north is going to be a lost cause, I saw another battle group coming. We're screwed. Get Gunther and Murlan and meet us in the castle. Close the gate after them. In there we can try and hold out for at least a few days." I raced into the castle and saw the hordes of women and children hiding against the walls. The archers in the castle had done a fantastic job at keeping the Drakes from entering the castle but that didn't mean one couldn't find its way in. "Get those children underground!" I yelled as I climbed to the top of the castle to survey the battle again.

Dwarves had taken on the strategy of launching themselves from burning roofs to mount the Drakes and take them down from the back. It was working except they were running out of roofs to jump from and too many Dwarves were being killed mid jump.

"Listen Dwarves! This is Danvel, the Dragon Slayer! Things look bleak right now but we must band together and fight back. We aren't going to lose to a bunch of dumb ass Wind Drakes." As I said this a particularly large Wind Drake came up behind me, arrows pouring into it from the archers. It ignored them.

"Your hubris will be your demise, Slayer," he snarled at me.

"And my sword will be yours." I launched myself at him and dug my sword into him. Despite the sword and the arrows, he kept fighting. We began to go into a free fall as I struck at him and he bit and clawed at me. We struck the ground hard, sending me flying off of the Dragon and into the building across from the castle. I got out and found that he was still alive, writhing on the ground. I pulled my sword from him and finished it off.

I marched back into the castle walls and yelled, "We're not going down without a fight!" The Dwarves all cheered and took up their weapons. "Let's beat some Dragon ass!" The Dwarves cheered again and began to line the top of the castle walls. I met up with Gunther and Murlan.

"How are you two doing?" I asked, pulling them into a castle hallway where they were housing the wounded. Gunther looked unusually worn down, and Murlan looked like his beard had gotten a little pale.

"I'm putting them down, Mr. Danvel, but they keep coming. That Dwarf, Caleb, and I have had to make three arrow runs already." His words came out a little labored. I chalked it up to his first real battle. Then I noticed his arm was bleeding where he had caught the dark energy blast.

"Where did you get that?" I asked as I pulled his arm up and covered it up using some medical cloth the Dwarves had. It looked worse than I was comfortable with.

"Some shrapnel got me from when a Wind Drake crashed into a house. Nearly took the whole thing down. I was lucky that I only got this," Gunther exclaimed.

"Don't get yourself killed, kid. What about you Murlan? You're looking pretty worse for the wear." Murlan sighed deeply and closed his eyes.

"I've run out of magic. I'm tapped dry and may have used too much of myself in the process." He sat down and almost fell over. I caught him and set him down on the ground. "I need a new power source."

"I don't know about you guys, but I killed a bunch of magical creatures recently that don't need their magic anymore. You do anything like that recently, Gunther?" Gunther smiled and patted Murlan on the shoulder.

"There's that and more magic to come," he replied as he grabbed his bow.

We were starting to exit the building when the ground began to shake and a great horn sounded in the distance. We exited into the courtyard as the shaking got more and more intense. "What the hell was that?" I yelled.

"It's James," a few Dwarves yelled back. Sure enough, about halfway through the town, a great Dragon rose from the ground. Almost as big as a Behemoth, James was the biggest Dragon I had ever seen. He took out several of the Wind Drakes and landed without harming a single building. It was a purposely graceful and terrifying move and the Wind Drakes acted accordingly.

With him, several other Earthwyrms, rose from the ground following suit on avoiding the buildings. The Earthwyrms had a brown and green hue that decorated their bodies and some had plants growing out of them. There legs were short so they stayed close to the ground it seemed. They took a defensive position, splitting the town in half; the Dwarves, Earthwyrms, and my team in the south and the Wind Drakes in the north.

"Citizens of Heartha, we have come to your aid. Wyrms! Half of you burrow escape routes for the inhabitants, the other half, hold this line!" James shouted. The Wyrms obeyed immediately and half of them disappeared as fast as they had come. I got Jeff, Gunther, and Murlan's attention and went to the castle gate. "Anyone who's coming let's go now!" I lifted the castle gate as several Dwarves and the team rushed out.

"Everyone else, stay safe and rely on each other," I said as an Earthwyrm burrowed its way up into the castle courtyard.

"I have these one's, go on ahead," he called. I crossed under the gate and let it fall. By the looks of things, the Earthwyrms were turning the tide of the battle, and at least rescuing the trapped families in the north. I caught up with the team just as they were reaching the line of Wyrms. "Need a helping hand?" I called to James just as he hurled a massive chunk of earth at an unexpecting Drake.

James turned to regard us and smiled. "Ah, Danvel. It is good to see you. We would love the assistance." Up close, James was even more intimidating than I imagined. His skin was mottled with mud, but his dark green color was still exposed. His had two fangs that protruded from his lower jaw that looked dangerously sharp. He also had two short horns that stuck out from his scalp above his eyes.

I was puzzled that he seemed to know me, but was glad to be well known. That painting and statue I commissioned must have been doing wonders for people recognizing me. Especially since they did such a great job on my beard! "Care to give me a lift?"

"It would be my pleasure," James said as he obliged by tossing me at a Dragon. The Wyrms were tossing pieces of the ground at the Drakes. The Drakes were responding by grabbing the Wyrms from the ground and carrying them into the occupied part of the city. No one saw what happened to them after that and no one wanted to.

The battle continued like this till almost night. Gunther and Murlan continued to battle as Jeff helped with evacuation. On my last jump up I saw another group of reinforcements coming in. I landed and bounded over towards James.

"James, there are reinforcements on their way. We can't keep this up," I yelled. Gunther ran up behind us.

"And we're completely out of arrows."

"We have to hold a little longer. There are still some families trapped! We have to hold," James yelled. He launched another piece of the ground at a group of Drakes, decimating them completely. "We can do this, Danvel. We aren't leaving anyone behind!"

"I have an idea," Gunther yelled as he ran back towards the castle. James and I continued to discuss what to do while fending off the Drakes.

I tackled a Drake that had dropped in behind us and took it down as James continued to hurl massive chunks of the ground. Somehow the ground around him was magically refilling itself as he tore from it. As I finished it off, Gunther ran back up with something in his hand.

"I have it," he yelled. "It's been talking to me since the desert, Mr. Danvel. It tells me it can save us. It can save us all. I have to make the hard decision." Gunther held his hand out revealing the still sheathed Muramasa. He placed his other hand on the sheath.

Gunther had an evil look in his eye that lasted for only a second as he held it in front of us. James began to growl; I assume sensing the dark energy that was emanating from the blade.

"Gunther! No!! It's lying to you! It's just trying to get out again," but it was too late. Gunther had unsheathed it. The dark energy burst forth knocking James and me over and several of the Wyrms were knocked back into the holes that they rose from.

I lifted my sword and got ready for a two front battle, but Gunther, or whatever he was now, took no notice of us. His eyes were dark and his armor turned as black as mine. He smiled a sinister smile then jumped into the fray with the Drakes and began decimating them.

"Quick! While they're distracted, get the rest of the survivors," James yelled, not missing the opportunity to save his people. We all joined in and got the last few families from the north side of town while MuraGunther continued fighting. He was uncanny. Taking down two or three Drakes in a single swipe and he was able to jump high enough that it looked like he was flying!

I ran into the north side of town plowing through some of the unaware Drakes. They seemed to be searching for the last of the survivors like we were. I took them down quickly before they could alert anyone else. Then I heard a woman cry, "Please help us, they found us!" I rushed over to find three Drakes cornering her and a small child. Two Earthwyrms popped their heads up out of holes they had silently dug behind the Drakes.

As the Drakes were about to make their move, the two Wyrms grabbed their tails and pulled them underground. I didn't want to see what would become of them. The third one turned his head around to see what happened only to find my sword in between his eyes. I went over to protect them when another Wyrm rose up from the ground. "Follow me, Dwarves. I will lead you to safety."

I searched the town for a few more minutes before returning to James. James was using those big fangs of his to take down a nearby Drake. He was also harboring a large gash on his side. By the bodies lying around him, I imagine that they had just unleashed a desperate strike.

"We got them all," I reported to James. Above the din of ongoing battle, a pair of beating wings could be heard. It grew louder every second and soon was louder than the sounds of the battle "What is that. It sounds like a thousand Wind Drakes just showed up out of nowhere!" I screamed.

"It couldn't be," James said with deep concern. He focused his eyes and then looked shocked. "I think it's Tiamat. EVERYONE GET UNDERGROUND QUICKLY." Everyone started to jump back in their holes. Murlan and Jeff ran to the one James was going for. The air started to become static with anticipation.

"But what about Gunther!" I looked up to the sky to see MuraGunther standing on a building sword ready to strike and Tiamat staring at him. The Wind Drakes had retreated leaving the sky mostly empty except for the smoke and Tiamat. Tiamat was an unreal size. Perhaps the oldest Dragon in existence. He made a Behemoth look small. Nearly twice the size of the Behemoth King. His white scales glimmered with the fire all around him and he smiled an evil smile.

"You have been foolish to stand against our might. It is time for the Dragon's to rule once again. James, how dare you fight against us? You soil your own species with your actions. I am here to take it all away," Tiamat send in a deep voice. His words dripped with death.

Murlan and Jeff, who had grabbed all of our supplies, started to push me into the hole as Gunther dove for him and Tiamat sucked in a deep breath. James grabbed all three of us, pulled us in, and with a wave of his hand sealed the hole. You could hear a mighty wind rush above us. It sounded like all the winds I had ever heard in my life all combined into one and brought down on us all at once. It was like an earthquake above ground.

We all huddled around each other til it was over, James standing at the entrance to the cave in case it needed resealed. "Should we go back up?" Murlan asked. He had his arms wrapped around his legs and his miniature hat was at his side. He was obviously shaken to know what had just happened… and he had lost his home.

"Gunther's gone," I said bleakly. "The magic I had shared with him just returned to me. "

"They'll be waiting for us anyways," James answered soberly. "I'll be sending my Wyrms to go evacuate the other cities to safer locations. I'm going to go to Salamandra to warn Fafnir and seek safe haven for my people. Danvel, I need you and your people to go back to Dragonia and warn Leviathan. I would go myself, but I doubt she'd believe me with the current war."

I didn't reply. I just sat there with Jeff leaning against me, thinking about the last few weeks. To James' credit, he showed absolutely no impatience and began burrowing a tunnel downwards.

Murlan stood off to the side, out of arm's reach. Apparently he was afraid I was going to act out.

The silence continued until James popped his head out of the tunnel he had dug and said, "Well aren't you coming?" He motioned us all to follow. We descended into the dark tunnel following James' footsteps. Eventually the tunnel broke into a massive well-lit cavern. Inside the cavern where the Dwarves of Heartha and what was left of the Earthwyrms.

All eyes turned to us as we entered the light. The Dwarves rushed over to greet us. Thanks and praise from all of them. James looked at us and smiled. "These are the people that you saved, Danvel, Murlan, and Jeff. You have our thanks and much, much more." It took some of the sting away from the death of Gunther, knowing how many we saved, but I still didn't want to talk. I simply bowed and went off to a corner in the room.

The Dwarves all gave me space and the only person that stayed near was Jeff. Soon an Earthwyrm came up carrying a bow. "Excuse me… I believe this was your friends. I found it on the battlefield before we retreated." He handed it to me and I stared at it.

"He was more than a friend… more like a son. Thank you." I grabbed the bow and gave him a pat on his side. I took the bow over to Jeff and hung it on the side of his armor. I jumped up and ran to where James was resting. Some of the Dwarves were tending to his wounds. His eyes were closed but I could tell he was aware of my presence. "Dragonia, then? How are we going to get there?" I asked, trying to get my mind off of failing Gunther.

James opened his eyes and stood up. "We have tunnels that go to the edge of Dragonia and in some cases to the coast. Those are more dangerous but they are the ones you need to go to." He stretched out a little, accidentally knocking a Dwarf over. "Thank you for accepting. I know you have had a terrible loss, but many more will be lost if you don't warn them."

"I understand what I need to do and why… what did you mean more dangerous?" Jeff and Murlan had joined us at this point and were listening intently.

"We haven't travelled into those tunnels for nearly a century, since the original Dragonia/Wyrmvale war started, and rumors state there is a powerful Dragon that made it its home. Whether it is true or not,

I don't know." He motioned for a Dwarf to come over. He had in his hand a glowing amulet. The Dwarf handed it to me.

"What's this?" I asked as I held it up. It had the same inlay as the Queen's amulet that she had used to curse Murlan but the gem inside was much different. It wasn't any type of gem I had ever seen before.

"It is a locator amulet. You ask it to take you to a location and its gem will shine in the direction that you need to go in. The gem is a fossilized Dragon scale with the magic still intact. Just ask it and it will lead you to Dragonia and beyond."

I stood up in front of all the Dwarves and raised my hands. "Dwarves and Wyrms. I must take my leave of you now! My adventure takes me to a new place. I wish you all well, and we shall see each other again soon!" The Dwarves all came over to wish us good luck and some tried to give us gifts from whatever they were able to bring during the battle. We, of course, refused.

"Come with me now," James said, waving us towards him. "I will show you to the start of the tunnel." James began burrowing into the side of the cavern, which to my surprise didn't affect the structural integrity of it a bit. He must have reinforced the cavern or knew what spots would affect it. It was nearly a mile away but James had dug to it in less than five minutes.

The tunnel we emerged in was nothing like we expected. It was paved and torches lined the walls already lit. "This is a surprising change," I commented. Jeff and Murlan were equally as amazed.

"All the tunnels of old were paved and permanently lit with magic. It would take an awful force to douse them. The Old Dwarves made these tunnels as a means of trade back before Dragonia provoked the war. These tunnels are older than I am, in fact," James explained. There were so many wonders in the world that had been buried because of the long war. And so many dangers it seemed, if this Dragon was making these tunnels his home.

"After we warn Leviathan and Dragonia, we'll make way to Salamandra to help with anything. We need to stick together you know? Survivors till the end!" I gave James a fist bump (yes, I invented that, too).

"Thank you, Danvel. We are all surely in your debt. I must hurry back now; we need to start moving the citizens of Heartha. Good luck to you all!" Murlan waved and Jeff whinnied his goodbye. We started to walk down the tunnel. It was truly a marvel. It must have taken them years to build the whole thing. That's when I remember the amulet.

"Amulet, thing…. uhhh… take us to Axdremaria!" The amulet didn't react. I decided that shaking it might help, but nothing.

"Stop that you imbecile," Murlan called. I glared at him because of his insult and he immediately backed down. "What I mean to say was… perhaps the magic user should take a look at the magic amulet?" I handed the amulet over but not without giving him a punch on his shoulder.

"Most amulets have a magical word. Let's try ALAKAZAM" The amulet stayed unresponsive. "Alright, that was just a joke. Let's try Agrophizit!" The amulet stayed unresponsive again. Then Murlan started shaking it.

"So, I'm an imbecile for shaking it, but you're allowed to!" I tackled Murlan and tried to get the amulet. He threw it to try and keep it away from me and it landed at Jeff's feet.

"Neighhhhhh," said Jeff causing the amulet to activate and point in the direction we wanted to go. "NEIGHHH," he said happily. I climbed off of Murlan, making sure to slap him one last time.

"See, Jeff figured it out! Better magician than some I know," I said, pointing to Murlan. Murlan grumbled but didn't reply. It was probably better that way. I placed the amulet around Jeff's neck. We continued following down the path which seemed to continue unendingly.

"Jeff, does that thing have an ETA for us," I asked. I didn't want to wander aimlessly without a goal to keep us steady.

"Neighhh," Jeff said into the amulet. The amulet reacted and shone brighter.

"Don-Don says that at the current rate of travel, your party will arrive in two days," the amulet announced. The amulet's name was apparently Don-Don. We continued down the path mostly in silence. It didn't take too long for us to get tired so we decided to make camp.

"You wouldn't happen to have an extra blanket?" Murlan asked. I had forgotten that he hadn't been able to save anything from his tent. I handed him Gunther's pack and supplies. Then I realized that Murlan had no reason to come with us.

"Murlan, can I ask you a question? Why did you come with us? Your home is in Wyrmvale and we haven't exactly been on the best of terms." I pulled out some food and started munching. I passed some of the food to Murlan and Jeff who gladly accepted.

"I think... I think I came because I wanted to do something right in the world for once. I keep messing things up. Insulting the Queen and getting cursed is just the tip of the iceberg. You guys, you seem to be on the right side of things."

"Well you did really well in the battle before. You saved lots of lives. The Dwarves weren't just thanking us." It took me a moment to notice that Murlan was crying. I stayed quiet to give him the time he needed. Time I needed to reflect. Eventually he got on his blanket and curled up. Jeff was already asleep so I decided to join them.

Chapter 11 - The Yellow Brick Tunnel

Earthwyrm Tunnels

"Don-Don, how much longer till Dragonia?" Murlan asked for the fiftieth time in the last hour. Apparently some of us weren't as used to walking as others. "I'm not as used to walking as you guys," he announced.

"Don-Don says if you keep asking then I'll stop showing the way." We all had a good laugh at the amulets response. A much needed laugh. The last time Murlan asked, the amulet had said five minutes. We had walked nearly most of the day, only stopping to eat and rest when Murlan couldn't take it anymore (which seemed like every ten minutes).

"We're almost there," I replied, slapping him on the back. He seemed to take heart from this and went from slouching to standing up straight.

"Destination reached. Please rate your experience at your nearest pub," Don-Don announced then shut off. This had left us in an awkward position, however. The tunnel branched off into five different directions. Jeff began neighing wildly into the amulet to no avail. Murlan joined in, neighing wildly as well.

"Let's take the center route. We should come up close to Axdremaria. Well closer than we are now. Let's get going!' I ran down the middle route and could hear Murlan and Jeff chasing after me. The tunnel began to change dramatically the farther we got into. The brickwork started to get sloppy and inconsistent and the lit torches became fewer and fewer.

"Stop," Murlan called from behind. I obeyed until he and Jeff caught up. Jeff seemed invigorated while Murlan was gasping for air. Jeff and I started play fighting while Murlan caught his breath. Eventually, he recuperated. "There is dark magic coming from up ahead. In fact, there are no more torches after this point."

I looked ahead to see that Murlan was telling the truth, it was pitch black. I grabbed one of the perpetual torches from the wall and started to move forward slowly. We had moved a little bit until we encountered a wall of black, much like when we had entered the Darkened Desert. When we stepped in, the torch went out immediately.

"Well that didn't work," I commented. I looked to my right and left but couldn't see Jeff or Murlan. "You guys still there?" No answer came from other side. I continued until I hit something solid and fell backwards.

"Lost, are we little one?" a voice called from not far ahead. "A good way to get yourself killed." I felt the solid mass in front of me start to move, slithering I assume.

"And calling me little one is a good way to do the same yourself. Where are my friends?" The monster recoiled at my confidence. He hissed deeply then moved his face close to mine.

"Which friends are you talking about? Jeff and Murlan? Or Gunther who you got killed!" His words bit me harder than I imagine he could. I fell backward at his accusation and grabbed for my sword. "You got him killed! How long will it be till the other two are dead as well?!" This time he actually bit at me and I raised my sword to block.

"I'll protect them with my life! Not just them! Everyone!" I began swinging my sword wildly in a panic and guilt, only striking the serpent once.

"And just like Gunther, you'll get them all killed. People die around you, little one. Your parents, the Behemoth's, Gunther." I swung my sword wildly again and when I was sure I was near the serpent's head I thrust forward into it. Except it wasn't the serpent's head, it was Gunther.

"Why, Danvel? Why did you kill me?" I pulled out my sword stunned but only for a second. I charged forward and stabbed past Gunther into the beast. The beast recoiled and hissed again.

"How did you see through my illusion, you vile creature!" The serpent sent its tail after me, knocking me back to the edge of the darkness, sending my sword flying, and then it wrapped its body around me, squeezing hard. "Now you shall pay for your insolence, Danvel!"

I tried to reach for my sword but the serpent had picked me up off the ground before I could get it back. "Gunther always called me, Mr. Danvel you slithering serpent. And I don't need a sword to defeat you!" I slammed my fists down onto the serpent's coils. After a few strikes, the serpent's hold began to loosen and I crawled free. I grabbed my sword and just as it went to snap at me, I dodged.

"You are a slippery thing, Danvel. But not as slippery as…" His mouth was suddenly preoccupied with the sword going through it. I pulled it out and dispatched of his head. Then the darkness cleared. The magical lanterns around me immediately turned back on. The serpent was big to be in these tunnels, but smaller than I had thought. Perhaps it had been projecting itself bigger like it was using the illusions of Gunther. Then I looked up and saw another section of darkness. Maybe this had just been a baby?

I rushed forward to hear Murlan crying again. Another serpent was talking to him. "Murlan the magician, most powerful in the land, but the only thing he can accomplish is the simple sleight of hand. Maybe if you hadn't done what you did, Danvel wouldn't be a kid. Maybe if you had used your head, they wouldn't all be dead." Murlan snapped at this.

"It was a new spell, completely untried! How did I know what it would do! If you can't push the boundaries of magic than you'll never be known as great!" That was when I ran in. I saw Murlan brimming with power, and then the serpent was gone. Not dead, just simply gone and the magic disappeared with it. It took a few moments for Murlan to calm down and then he noticed me.

"How... how long have you been standing there?" he asked a little frightened. Frightened of me or what he had just done, I don't know.

"I thought the only magic you could use was to make things Dwarven size?" I asked, suspiciously. Murlan sat down for a second and rested.

"I did. I just amped up the magic in the spell so it kept making it smaller till it was too small to contain the amount of magic it had in it." His words had a sort of edge to them and I knew that I shouldn't ask anymore.

"You didn't see Jeff did you?" I asked as I looked ahead and found no more walls of darkness. All the torches were lit along the tunnel and the brickwork seemed to normalize.

"Haven't seen him since you disappeared." I picked him up off the floor and we headed further down the tunnel. We found Jeff talking to another serpent and no darkness wall surrounding them.

"So you've travelled from Dragonia to Wyrmvale and now you're on your way back again in less than a month? That is a bit of travel. At least you had companions to travel with. Anytime I go anywhere my brothers are like 'go by yourself or are you a snakelet.' So I go and do my own thing. Siblings are difficult to deal with, especially when you have fifty of them. I'm the black sheep of them, as it were."

The serpent was stark black, so black that it seemed that the light around them was absorbed into nothingness, much like his brothers. They had scales like a Dragon, but they weren't like any Dragon I had ever seen before.

"Neighhhh," Jeff said in a sadder tone. Murlan and I walked closer to them, hoping our presence would be noticed and it was. Jeff stood up immediately and excitedly while the serpent simply turned its head to take us in.

"I suppose this is Murlan and Danvel. Jeff has rave things to say about you, Danvel. Did you have any trouble with my brothers? I hope you gave them what they deserved; the fear mongers," the serpent said kindly. Unlike his brothers this serpent had no malice in his voice.

"That we did, kind serpent. I suppose Jeff has filled you in on our adventure," I said, stepping forward to show no fear of the serpent.

"I am Simon, a terrible serpent name. My mother has no ability for naming anything," he said in a matter of fact tone of voice. "I hear you are heading to Axdremaria, or as we called it when I was born, the city of Leviathan. You picked the right tunnel as far as direction, but you also picked the wrong tunnel as far as Dragons. This tunnel has us three brothers and my mother, one of the last great Chaos Dragons. The other tunnels house just my brothers."

"If you're a Chaos Dragon then why help us?" I asked, putting my hand on my sword for a second.

"What could be more chaotic than doing the opposite of what I was supposedly born for? It makes no sense at all. Now go along before my mother comes and finds I am the only one alive. She is not to be trifled with. My brothers preyed on your fears but she would prey upon your soul." We took his warning wholeheartedly; if his brothers could get into our brain that easy, what was she capable of?

We continued further down the tunnel until the brickwork became inconsistent again. Now understanding that we were dealing with a Chaos Dragon, it began to make sense. Then we ran into the wall of black again. "Shall we?" I asked to none of them in particular; we had to go.

I stepped in and the first thing that I noticed was the absolute rank smell. It was as if the mother had eaten half of her victims and left the other half to rot. This was confirmed by Murlan tripping over a corpse… or half of one. There wasn't any sign of the mother, however.

We continued on, weapons at the ready. With each step it seemed like the smell intensified. A voice called from further down the tunnel. It was a little girl. "Help me, please! I was taken from my parents and don't know where I am." We raced after the sound, tripping over the occasional corpse. "I don't want to be eaten, please!" The closer we got, the further it seemed to get away.

"We're being toyed with," Murlan stated. "The mother is probably making that voice to lure us into her trap." He stopped running.

I stopped with him. "But what if she actually has a little girl and is just pulling her further and further into the tunnel. We can't just stop and hope for the best, trap or not." Murlan didn't seem to want to agree, but eventually he caved. We continued our race towards the voice until we noticed that the torches were gradually coming back on.

There the mother stood in front of us. Nearly three times the size as her kids, the mother was impressive. She looked to be ten feet thick and fifty long. Her scales seemed to glow in comparison to her sons. I pulled my sword and got ready. Then she shook her tail and her scales turned outward into spikes. "I see the killers of my sons

have come to take the mother on. Well I shall give you no quarter."
Not that I thought she was going to anyways.

Just like that she was coming at us. I shoved Murlan back as
she struck Jeff and me. My armor held so I knew Jeff's would. She
pinned us against the wall with her body and went to strike at
Murlan. Murlan held his staff up at the last moment causing the
mother to bite down on it instead of him. Instead of snapping like I
expected, the staffs point pierced through the top of the mother's
mouth. The staff stayed stuck in her mouth because of the knotted
end.

She shrieked in pain, letting us on the ground. I took the
opportunity to drive my sword deep into her side, causing her to
ooze a rank black blood. It was noxious to breathe in, causing us all
to cough in fits. I struck again in the middle of a coughing fit,
making thing worse. The mother started to strike against the walls,
causing the bricks to fall down and the cave to collapse partially on
top of her.

"You vile insects! You sting at me but I will sting back!" She
flung her body up, causing the rubble to pile on top of us. Murlan lay
unconscious while Jeff and I dug ourselves out from it. When I

cleared it all from me, the mother was waiting for me and snapped at me. I caught her mouth with my hands and tried with all my might to keep them open. She was stronger than anything I had experienced before! It took all my strength to keep them open and not snapping at me.

Jeff arose from the rubble and quickly latched on to the end of Murlan's staff, still hanging out of the top of the mother's head. Jeff slammed it back into her mouth then pulled it out the top of her head. A large amount of her mouth came with it, shattering bone and scale. Then we were blown back by a force of dark energy. A voice came into our heads. "You haven't won yet, insects."

When we stood up we were in Dragonia again, but it wasn't a place I recognized. It was a warm night by the way that the air smelled. It brought back memories of being a kid. Maybe that's it was supposed to do to get me off guard. I grabbed my sword from my feet and stood at the ready. Suddenly a dark Dragon came barreling at us. It passed through us but began destroying the village around us. A man ran out of a house wielding a familiar sword.

It was my father. He stood as tall as I was, well as tall as I used to be. I looked at his face and a sense of longing came over me and not caused by the Chaos Dragon. It was the longing to know my family. My heart felt a sense of sorrow for a moment, but I quickly swallowed it and took in the rest of the scene.

The Dragon continued to rage around. My father went at the beast, mortally wounding it but the beast lunged forward in one last strike killing my father and landing on top of our house, crushing my mother. It was a tale I had been told many times. I rushed over to see my father. His face was almost identical to mine and I felt the sorrow build again; not just for his deaths but Gunther's, too. I swallowed it again.

"Doesn't it sting? To watch the loss of your family? The loss of your childhood? Isn't it soul crushing to witness it?" a voice, I assume the mothers, spoke in my head. The voice was coaxing yet still vile. I responded by laughing. "You laugh at your family's death?"

"No. I laugh at your attempts to use it against me. I came to terms with my family's death a long time ago. I can see through your illusions." I threw my sword in front of me and then, suddenly, the illusion and the darkness were gone. Nearly thirty five feet in front of me, the mother lay dead on the floor with my sword sticking out of her head.

"Neighhhh," Jeff called.

"I know! That was a good sword throw! I knew those sword throwing lessons would come in handy sometime. Waste of money you said." I said as a half joke. Jeff gave me a knowing look. A look saying that he understood my pain. I tore the sword from her head and stabbed it in again. It's always good to be sure about these things. Jeff came over and kicked her. He knew the drill.

We ran back to where Murlan was lying unconscious still. We cleared off the rubble and drug him to his feet. I threw him over Jeff and we hightailed it away from the dead mother. The smell was getting worse by the second.

Eventually we reached the end of the tunnel which was completely blocked. I looked around and hoped to find a lever, but only found a skeleton. Jeff changed the skeleton's body into a comedic position in an attempt to cheer e up, and it worked. Murlan was just stirring as I was feeling up the wall for a secret switch.

"A dead end? Do you think the Earthwyrms sealed it when the war started?" He asked when he stood up. "Also, what happened to the mother Chaos Dragon?"

"Oh, we finished her off. She did not know who she was messing with," I said while Jeff and I flexed repeatedly. I acted like I was throwing my sword and Jeff mimicked the Dragon. Murlan walked over stunned at our actions and that's when he laid eyes on the skeleton.

"Did this man die in the ridiculous position? It looks like he was grabbing his buttocks as he died. Preposterous!" Jeff began laughing hysterically as I returned to checking out the wall.

"It surely is a preposterous way to die. Perhaps he was stabbed in the butt. And I'm not seeing any secret way to open it." Murlan came over and double checked it.

"I concur, so what do we do?"

"Stand back," I said. I unleashed a haymaker causing the dirt covering the hole to burst outward and fill the tunnel with light. We covered our eyes but were blinded by the sudden natural light. It took us a few minutes to regain our senses and then we stepped outside. As quickly as the light came, the rain came afterward, drenching us all. "Yep, we're in Dragonia again. About two days out from Axdremaria if it keeps raining like this. Let's freaking go."

We continued on until we reached a nearby town.

Dragonia

Cordelia

Early Morning

The town of Cordelia was one of the more rural towns in Dragonia. There was only one fountain and none of the fanciful buildings that Axdremaria had. It happened to also be where I grew up. After my parents had died, I came to live with an aunt on my mother's side. Sadly, she had passed while I was out on another adventure. The life of an adventurer often means missed time with loved ones. After her death, I tried to leave flowers on her grave every year. This sometimes meant trekking across more than one continent.

"So how long until we reach Axdremaria from here?" Murlan asked. He had slept nearly the whole time since we arrived yesterday till today.

"It will be less than a day. Maybe five hours at the most. It all depends on the rains. Last time we trekked through Dragonia, the rains were unusually strong and it took us twice as long to reach the border than we expected. Jeff came up behind us carrying a huge sack. "Did you get everything we needed?" Jeff shook his head a little too excitedly.

I opened the sack to find a massive amount of apples, Jeff's favorite. "You're lucky that we can eat these. Last time he bought tons of dried oats which aren't exactly appetizing or filling."

"Neighhhh," Jeff said excitedly as he pulled out an apple and ate it rapidly. I took one too and began eating it.

"You guys go on ahead of me using this trail right here," I said as I pointed westward. "Jeff should remember how to get there. I'll catch up; I just need to pay my respects." Jeff and Murlan followed my instructions and went up the path I directed them to.

I went the opposite way to the other side of town where the graveyard was. It was a well maintained graveyard and my family was lucky to have someone who took so good care of their resting place. As I passed grave keeper Colesmith's house, I made sure to leave a small sack of money for him.

And then I was there. Beside each other lay my parents and my aunt on the right of them. All taken too soon. "Oh, if you could only see things now, Dad. The temple is nearly cut off from the world and a new Dragon War has started. I just hope you're proud of how I'm handling everything." I pulled three bouquets of flowers from my pack and placed them at each grave. "I hope you're all proud," I said as a tear or two escaped my eye. "Speed us along now."

I dashed off to meet up with Jeff and Murlan. It didn't take me long to catch up. I looked up and there was sun shining and no rain in sight. "This is weird," I commented as I got in step with them.

"What's that?" Murlan asked. He had clearly been preoccupied.

"There's no rain! It's the nicest day I can remember on the countryside of Dragonia." We enjoyed the nice weather and kept a steady pace for the rest of the trip. Instead of the five hours that it would've probably taken us because of the rain, we reached Axdremaria in two. That was when I realized what today was. Torrent day.

Torrent day was twice a month in Axdremaria. It was a day where everyone was supposed to stay inside so Leviathan could bring a torrential downpour on the city to clear the muck and filth away. It rained harder than anywhere else in Dragonia and anyone who set foot in it had the chance to be washed away. I hated this day. You could see the curtain of rain pouring down in front of you.

We stepped in and were drenched immediately. My beard hung lower than it ever had before. Murlan wasn't faring well either. His miniature hat was drooping and his long beard seemed to weigh him down. Jeff didn't seem to mind at all and was splashing into the puddles. All the houses had their lights out so we couldn't find shelter with anyone.

We kept trudging along until we came across the Leviathan Pub. "Freaking pub. I do not want to see Gale like this."

"Neighhh," Jeff said stubbornly.

"Fine, fine," I said as I opened the door and we walked in. The bar was completely empty except for Gale and the roaring fireplace. She rushed over to us with blankets.

"Danvel! Oh my gosh! You look like you've been through a lot." I was surprised at the concern in her voice. She wrapped the blanket around me. "Come over to the fireplace with me." She led me over to it and sat down.

"So you're nice to me when no one else is around," I sniped. She was taken aback by my statement but then her face took on a kinder look.

"I was mad at you Danvel! You leave on these adventures without telling me and expect me to be okay with it. The last one you came back half your size! One of these days you're just not going to come back. I couldn't handle that!" I tried to say something back, but I didn't have anything to say. She was right.

I pulled her close and gave her a hug. "You're right, Gale. I should have told you. But it's not like I exactly chose to be what I am. People depend on me. People need me! Especially now," I said in a hushed tone.

"What do you mean, especially now?"

"A Dragon war has started. It's why we came back. The Drakes attacked Heartha, the capital of Wyrmvale. The Dwarf Queen is dead. Tiamat surfaced and blew the whole city away," I said squeezing her arm gently.

She looked around at Jeff and Murlan and made a face. "What happened to your friend?" I looked away at the mention.

"Gunther didn't make it. He was on the surface when Tiamat blew the town over." I put my head down and she placed her hands on my shoulders. Jeff and Murlan came over to join us.

"Neighhh," Jeff said meekly.

"Yes, Jeff. I was mad at you too," Gale replied. "But now things are fine. Who's this new fellow though?"

"I am Murlan, the wizard," he said with a bow. His sopping wet beard fell to the floor and left a massive puddle when he rose.

"You mean you're the rat bastard who turned my Danvel into a midget?" She began smacking a Murlan wildly.

"It's fine, Gale," I said, stepping in front of her and grabbing her arms. "It wasn't his fault. He was cursed." Murlan walked away warily, rubbing his arm. Then the doors burst open.

"This damned rain will be the death of me! Why did you bring us out in this, Lynnaedra?" It was Hourig! Lynnaedra and Aturdokht followed behind him.

"I told you when we left the inn that Danvel was sighted entering here! Speak of the devil," She said as she saw me. We all exchanged warm pleasantries and sat down at a large table.

Gale brought us all over some mead and sat down with us. "What brings you back here, Danvel? And looking the same. Where's Gunther! Did you find yourself?"

I filled all of them in on the whole journey. The Behemoths, Muramasa, the Dragon King, and Wyrmvale. They were astonished at the events. "Poor Gunther. He was a good companion to have on an adventure," Hourig stated. It was probably the best compliment I could imagine him giving. "To Gunther," he said as he raised his glass. We all raised ours and drank deeply in remembrance.

"What brought you three back to Axdremaria?" I asked as I finished my glass. "I thought you had an adventure yourselves."

"We began to ask around Earwyna about the appearance of the lightning wizard and it seemed to coincide with the Desert of Rebirth being overcome with darkness," Lynnaedra explained. "So we decided to come back here and investigate. We didn't find anything, but we were put on the waiting list to meet with Leviathan. Speaking of which, how do you plan on meeting her to warn her about Tiamat?"

"I just need to get in the castle. There is a horn that can be blown in case of emergencies. But there's no getting into the castle in this weather. Leviathan usually moves the castle further out to sea during the downpours." I sat in thought for a moment till Hourig arose from his seat.

"I shall throw you, Danvel! No storm can match the might of a throw from a Fire Dragon!" Hourig puffed up making his inner glow rise to the surface. He shone much more brightly than I had seen before. "Let's get to it, kid! We have a war to prevent!" Just like that he was gone.

I turned to Gale and ran my hand across her face. "I'll be back shortly. Wait for me?"

"As long as you don't get yourself killed," she replied with a smile. "Jeff you best keep your lazy ass aware and keep Danvel safe!" Jeff raced out the door in front of me, peeked his head back in, and waved me out. I implored everyone else to stay. Everyone, except for Lynnaedra, listened.

As soon as I stepped outside I was drenched again. We walked the small distance to the bridge to the castle and stopped. The bridge was no longer attached to the castle. The castle was standing steady about three hundred feet away. "How the hell do you expect to throw me that far?"

"Wait and see, boy!" Hourig picked me up with one arm and launched me as hard as he could…. just as the rains and wind shifted. I immediately blew back into him, knocking him over into Jeff which sent him tumbling.

"I just saw," I yelled. I picked myself up and helped Hourig up. Jeff came prancing up with an angry look on his face.

"Quiet now! I'm concentrating," Lynnaedra announced. Right before us, the rain in between us and the castle began turning into a stream of water leading to it. "There! That is how you shall cross. If Hourig wishes, he can throw you into the stream." Before I had a chance to object, Hourig had me off the ground and into the stream.

"Off with you now! No time to lose!" I began tumbling wildly through the air until the stream threw me right into the castle wall… hard. I was dazed and stumbled backward, almost falling off of the castle platform. I caught myself and turned around, giving them all a big thumbs up.

Like I mentioned before, Leviathan Castle paled in comparison to the Dwarf Castle. But I guess it didn't matter anymore since the Dwarf Castle didn't exist. The castle had a blue hue and, you guessed it, fountains everywhere. Water was flowing through the walls as well. The guards that were usually posted at the door must have taken shelter inside because of the weather.

I walked in, out of the weather, and found that the floor inside was wet, and the torches weren't lit. "Hello," I called out, but no one answered. I kept moving forward, feeling the wall for direction. I continued forward until I tripped over something and felt that the floor was wet from the rain again. I pulled the object near to a window and found out it wasn't water on the floor, it was blood. I had tripped over a dead guard.

I searched the guard for a dry torch and as luck would have it, he had one. I lit it and looked around. There were dead guards everywhere. I rushed up through the castle, not finding a single living person the whole time, and then I made it to the throne room. Baron Dexter lay dead on his throne.

I checked his body and it was still warm. I raced up to the lookout to where the horn was located and blew it. A great blast of sound emanated from it. Almost immediately the sky began clearing. I looked behind me and the townspeople all flooded out from their houses. Lynnaedra, Hourig, and Jeff were still at the bridge.

Behind me the water started to bulge. Out of the bulge rose Leviathan. She was an impressive Dragon. She rose to the top of the castle to face me. Her body went on for longer than I could see. Her scales shone a deep cerulean and her eyes were decorated with an even deeper red. She was about a quarter of the width of the castle. Then she rose up even higher and looked down at me.

"Who calls Leviathan? Who dares disturb Torrent day?" she hissed. Her body shook, causing excess water to rain down from her.

"It is I, Danvel the Dragon Slayer. I come with grave news from Wyrmvale that James has asked me to deliver for him." Leviathan laughed at this. It was a cruel laugh, full of malice and spite. She apparently thought this was funny.

"James, that coward. Couldn't deliver the message himself so he had a pitiful humanoid do it for him," she spat. She also apparently didn't like James. She didn't seem like she liked anything.

"That coward is seeing his people to safety. They were attacked by the Wind Drakes and Tiamat leveled the city of Heartha. If it weren't for me and my team, the Dwarves of the city would have surely been wiped out. James asked me to return here to warn you in case Tiamat attacked here." Leviathan's eyes narrowed at my statement and she got closer, baring her fangs.

"If it weren't for you, Danvel, you wretched Dragon Slayer. Tiamat won't attack here because he and I are on the same side. The side against humans!" I placed my hand on my sword as soon as she said it.

"You wretched serpent! How dare you?" I screamed.

"How dare I? How dare you humanoids! How dare you Dragon Slayers? We used to rule this domain completely but now we share it with your rotten ilk. And you Danvel should be dead already! You thought that a Dragon suffering from Arcane Rot could have killed your father so easily? Even I know that your father was a better Slayer than that." I was taken back by her statement. Of course it had to be a Dragon with Arcane Rot.

"We were set to kill your whole line that night. If it was for interference from the patron Dragon of Wyrmvale, Adhamhnan, you would be dead too! We besieged that village with an army of loyal Water Dragons. Your father was fighting well, but even he couldn't hold us off for long. We disposed of him and your mother and just as we were about to kill you, Adhamhnan rose from the ground and fought off all the Water Dragons. I killed him for his transgressions."

I fell onto the ground from the shock of what she was saying. My whole family killed by the Water Dragons. I blamed the Earthwyrms for killing them but they were the ones who saved me. "I thought the next Earthwyrm patron would be more obedient but James was even worse than Adhamhnan," Leviathan continued. "When we moved to finish the Dragon King's line, James killed all of the Water Dragons and disappeared before I could find him."

"That was when we decided we had to be rid of the Wyrms. It's why we started the war again and blamed it on the Wyrmvalians. They were too compatible with the humanoids. Tiamat set himself to wipe out the Dwarves and whatever earthborn creatures might dwell in Wyrmvale. Salamandra had to go, too. Fafnir resisted all attempts we made for him to join us. That's why we sent something special after them… Ice Dragons. All things would have been going smoothly," she said, her eyes narrowing on me.

"Then you began to meddle," she accused. "I cut off the Dragon Slayer Temple and Dragon Temple off from the rest of the world and yet you still managed to make it there. You bested the wizard I sent after you. You even bested Muramasa, the ancient evil. You saved the Behemoths and their immense knowledge. You saved the Dwarves and James from sure death. But now, Danvel? You and all of these people will die!"

Behind Leviathan, a large wave began to form. The wave began to rise continuously and soon became the biggest tidal wave I had ever seen. As the tidal wave began to grow I clamored to the top of the castle. Soon the tidal waves shadow encapsulated all of Axdremaria with its shadow. "Die, you filth," she screamed. Just as the wave began to descend, I launched myself at her, sword drawn.

Chapter 12 - Under the Sea

Axdremaria

Under The Sea

Sometimes I have good ideas. Sometimes I don't. Fighting the so-called Lord of the Seas while in the sea might not have been my best. I spent most of my time holding on to my sword which was dug into her neck... or belly... or whatever it was dug into. The other time was spent trying not to drown. She kept diving in and out of the water, trying to get me to fly off. Then I remembered. I'm really strong!

While I held onto the sword with one hand, I began punching right beside my sword. If she was like any other creature, it should have hurt. And like I predicted, she felt it. She let out a long howl and raised her body from the sea. I took stock of where I was and decided that I don't know where the heck I had stabbed her in. At least it seemed to be bleeding pretty badly. I ripped out my sword and stabbed it back into her nearby before she plunged us back under again.

That's when I found out her howl in pain did more than give me satisfaction. Water Dragons, I assume the ones loyal to her cause, were racing towards me. I ripped my sword from her side, leaving a huge gash, and played a game of whack the Dragon as I swam for the surface. When I finally broke the surface I found that I was completely surrounded, but Leviathan was nowhere to be found.

I kept swimming and fighting with the Water Dragons. However well I was doing, it was only a matter of time before they would overtake me in their element. Then I saw a massive wave coming towards me. Except it wasn't a wave… it was the trunk of Leviathan's body charging at me. I tried to swim away but I knew there was no way to avoid it.

She struck me hard sending me up on the shore and into a tree. It didn't matter how good my armor was, it didn't protect me from that kind of impact. I could feel some of my ribs break. I tried to stand and a wave of pain ran through me and I threw up. I fell back down on the ground hacking a little bit. I grabbed my sword and used it to help me get to my feet. Leviathan's body was still on the shore and trying to slither away.

Despite the reservations my body had, I began to run at her. I launched myself off the ground and drove my sword deep into her body, hitting bone. I smashed my left hand on the butt of the sword to drive it through the bone, but effectively breaking my left hand at the same time. I heard both of our bones crunching when I hit it. Her howls could be heard from wherever she was.

Her body stopped moving when I broke the bone so I decided to take advantage of it. I began to hack away at her trunk and after a few moments separated the top and bottom half of her. It wasn't the most pleasant of experiences with a large amount of blood being spilt around and on to me. She howled again and then the Water Dragons started to show up on the shore. I retreated further back to the tree line; putting some distance between the increasing numbers. When they stopped coming I think I counted an even fifty.

So I attacked them. One down, my sword through his head. Two, a sword in its torso as it leapt at me. Three, I stabbed my sword down into it. Four, I grabbed the top of its head with my left hand, not a great idea, and ripped off its jaw with my right. Five, I gave a punch right between its eyes. Six, seven, eight, nine, I swung my sword in a massive arc. Another bad idea.

I fell to the ground and nearly passed out from the pain. The Water Dragons surrounded me. I raised my sword for one last hurrah when they all turned around. I looked up and saw a group attack them. It was Jeff and the rest of the gang! I tried to stand up and join them but I could barely move. I looked up to see that Leviathan had climbed up on top of the castle and behind her another tidal wave was forming.

"Hourig," I called out into the battle. My voice sounded meek against the din of the battle and even meeker than I thought it should. A path appeared before me as Hourig killed whatever Dragon he needed to get to me.

"Well you're looking a little worse for wear, Danvel. We need to get you out of here!" He tried to pick me up but I stopped him.

"Can... can you throw me to the castle," I said with labored breaths. I pointed over to where Leviathan was and at the newly forming tidal wave. I coughed one more time.

"I don't think it's the best idea, Danvel. I should go instead," he argued.

"It's me or no one, Hourig. Plus you won't make it running there. There would be too much ground to cover. You need to throw me. Plus if I fail, you need to protect the people." He stared at me in what I hope was admiration, or maybe it was pity. Thankfully, he picked me up and threw me like I wanted.

It reminded me of when I launched myself out of the catapult but with much less of the terror. The lack of terror was either because I knew I was going to die or I knew I had an important task to do. I pushed the specifics from my mind, the castle was getting closer. I landed in a roll and immediately stood up and dashed for the door, sword drawn. Each step seemed like I was carrying a Behemoth on each leg, but I pushed on.

I ran up the tower to where the summoning horn rested and where Leviathan was hovering over. I walked through the door and took stock of the situation. Leviathan looked as bad as I did. I could only assume she was dying from the wounds I had given her. Drool was leaking from her and her cerulean color had changed to white. Despite her near death, the second tidal wave was still forming. It was almost half of the size of the last one.

I gave myself some distance and did a running jump at the castle wall, kicking at it and jumping off at Leviathan. I thrusted my sword first right into her throat and knocking her off of the castle. We began a freefall, but Leviathan offered no resistance and the tidal wave continued to grow. We hit the water with a loud crash (and even more pain). Leviathan didn't react. She was dead and yet the tidal wave kept growing. I swam back to the surface and saw that it had grown even greater than the one before it.

The castle began to sink without the power of Leviathan but the tidal wave just moved forward and then smashed over the town. I swam as fast as I could over to the shore to avoid the wave but my body didn't afford me much speed. Eventually I made it to the shore to find Jeff waiting for me. He helped me climb out of the water.

He pulled me into a ditch covered by a tree and let the tidal wave wash over us. It was the most pleasant of unpleasant experiences I had experienced today. "Neigh... neighhhh," he said as I rose from my feet.

"What?! No!" I yelled as I ran back towards town. Limped was more like it. I found the Leviathan Pub completely smashed from the first tidal wave and even more so from the second. I began throwing rubble in every different direction. "Gale! Where are you?" I yelled. I kept throwing debris out of the way till I found her. She lay limp with a huge gash across her torso. I checked her pulse; her heart was still beating strong, but with a wound like that, I knew that wouldn't last for long.

I picked her up with my right arm and pulled her from the wreckage. Murlan and Jeff ran up behind me. "Murlan, you have to help her!"

"I can't! I just make things small, remember?"

"Well make the damn cut small," I screamed. Murlan closed his eyes in concentration. He began to glow with power and simultaneously Gale's cut began to shrink. She started to wake up and I set her on the ground... then I passed out.

Hopefully Axdremaria

I woke up tied to a cot and out of my armor. Not one of the ways I usually like to wake up. I looked around and found that there were other people on cots, not tied up I might add. I was in an infirmary, or a tent used as an infirmary. When I looked around I could count almost fifty bodies lying unconscious. My ribs still ached terribly but my hand seemed to have recovered nicely.

"Umm, excuse me," I called out. Jeff perked his head up from beside me and did an excited spin. He ran out and then back in with Murlan.

"Thank goodness you've finally awaken, Danvel. I thought for sure that you weren't going to make it," Murlan exclaimed as he began untying me.

"Why the hell am I tied up? Where's Gale at?" I asked bewildered.

"You're tied up because you launched yourself in furors because of fever dreams. After we laid you down to rest an infection set in and you had an awful fever. If it weren't for Galen and some healers, you surely would have died. You had internal injuries that were beyond most healers but Galen gave us one of his Phoenix feathers." I stood up and fell to the ground almost immediately. My ribs were surely still aching. Jeff and Murlan helped me to my feet.

"Where is Gale?" I asked more determinedly. Jeff let me lean on him as Murlan guided us outside.

"We'll take you to her now." Murlan led us outside and to one of the few buildings left standing in sight. There was destruction everywhere.

"How many buildings were left standing?" It was amazing and scary to see what one Dragon was able to do to so many people. I bet if I had seen what had become of Heartha, I'd have felt even worse that Tiamat was still out there.

"Most of the buildings that are still standing are the older ones, back from when Humanoids and Dragons were still at war.

They were built with tidal waves in mind and built to survive. The Temple of Christ was still standing, but I hear those Christians know something about building a firm foundation," Murlan answered.

"I couldn't stop her," I said dejectedly. We entered to find a packed house. Displaced families were huddled around their small sections and looked like that hadn't slept in weeks.

"Nothing could have stopped her, Danvel. But if you hadn't done what you did, all of these houses would have been destroyed and all the people with it. You saved more than half of the people in Axdremaria." It was hard to feel good about what he said. If only I had arrived sooner, or saw the signs.

"Neigh!" Jeff said with pride. We reached the back of the building and on a cot sat a small woman with a bandage across her chest. She turned around and smiled and immediately I knew it was her. I assume Murlan's magic had the same effect on her as it did me, but it must have affected her after her wound shrank. I limped over to her and gently embraced her. No words had to be said. Jeff and Murlan left us.

"I'm so glad to see you're okay," she said with a tear in her eye. "And now we're the same size!" I kissed her hard. She kissed back. It was the only response I needed. We sat there and enjoyed each other's company for some time. Then I rose and held out my hand.

"Come with me?" I asked, already knowing the answer. She took my hand and I led her out of the building and to the bridge to where the castle used to be. We sat staring at the ocean with our legs hanging off of the bridge. Only the tallest towers of the castle still stood visible.

"What do we do now, Danvel?" she asked softly as she laid her head on my shoulder.

"We as in you and I or the people of Axdremaria?" Both questions were valid.

"You and I, for now. I know you can't stay here. People still need helping. I can't leave here now. I want to help with the rebuilding." I smiled at her statement. I was happy that she understood that I was a major player in all of this and that my need to help people was more than just about myself. Nothing like tragedy to bring people together.

"I actually had something for this moment, but I don't know where my pack got to. Probably lost in all the wreckage." As usual with things like this, Jeff came by dragging my pack behind him. He gave it to me and left. "Did I ever tell you that I love that Sleipnir?"

I dug the ring out of my pack and got it ready. "In fact, have I ever told you, I love you, Gale? I know this isn't the most ideal time to ask this type of question. I might die tomorrow, but that's why I need to know. Will you marry me?" I pulled out the ring and presented it to her.

"You know the answer is yes, Danvel," she said as tears welled up in her eyes. I slipped the ring on and she gave me a massive hug.

"Gently," I said as she squeezed harder than I would have liked. She let go as I started coughing. I whistled and Jeff came prancing over with a sly look on his eye. He definitely already knew. I gave him a hug and messed up his mane.

"Jeff, get the whole team and assemble them here. Galen and Darren, if he's still breathing." Jeff obeyed and went on his way. Gale and I sat on the bridge, holding hands and waiting. Eventually, Jeff showed up with everyone I asked for. I stood up slowly, Gale helping me.

"Everyone! We suffered a disaster here, but we averted a calamity for all of Dragonia. The continent is still facing a dire threat, however. Tiamat and his forces are still out there, and Leviathan said that Ice Dragons are on their way to Salamandra to attack and potentially kill Fafnir and the whole Salamander race. The Great War is over, and we are faced with a Dragon war like we have never heard of. We need to put aside the differences of this continent and any of our peoples and join together to fight. Who's with me?" I cheered. Everyone cheered in agreeance, even Darren, who seemed surprised that I included him.

"I have tasks for each of you that need done before we can wage war on our terms. First, Lynnaedra, you are our Water Dragon contact. In fact, according to me, you are now the queen of the Water Dragons. We need to know who was loyal to Leviathan's plan and who wasn't. Those that opposed it are with us and need to be gathered here to protect the town." Lynnaedra nodded in agreement and trotted off.

"Darren, I need you to find whatever capable men you can and protect the town as well. I'm sure that you already sent men to other towns to get help in rebuilding, but we need an army. You're the Baron now. The highest knight that isn't deployed. Bring them home and get them ready for a different kind of war." Darren looked frightened by what I said.

"But why me, Danvel? I'm just a knight who makes up stories to sound like a hero," he replied.

"Well now is the time to prove that you're the hero that your stories say you are. Can I rely on you?" I asked as I put my hand on his arm. It would've been his shoulder, but he was tall!

"I'll do it, Danvel!" He raced off into a building nearby and came out with his sword and armor.

"Hourig and Aturdokht? I need the fastest route to Salamandra. It seems that Murlan, Jeff, and I need to stop some Ice Dragons and could use some help."

Aturdokht kind of shrugged but Hourig puffed up like usual. "Boy, we'll get you there faster than a wind sprite passes gas!" I patted him on the shoulder.

"I have no doubt, Hourig. No doubt at all." I sent them off. "Jeff and Murlan... get our supplies ready; we need to leave as soon as possible." They both went on their way leaving me with Gale and Galen.

"I suppose you have some orders for me, too," Galen asked with a sneer.

"Just a question, Galen. I heard that you helped save me. Doesn't sound like something you'd do. Selfless, that is. In fact, I'd almost say you'd probably had an ulterior motive." Galen chuckled at this.

"Someday, you'll learn that nothing I did was selfish or selfless, Danvel. It was all a calculated risk. It was all part of a plan. Whatever you do Danvel, don't stop." Galen put his hand on mine then walked away. I tried to race after him, but my aching ribs started to flare up. He turned the corner and Gale helped me limp after him. When we finally rounded the corner, he and his shop, which miraculously survived the attack unscathed, were missing.

"I really freaking hate this type of stuff," I said as I shook my head. "More questions than answers half of the time." We walked back to her cot and sat down. Despite the misery around us, and all I had just been through, I felt happier than I had in a long time. She looked at me for a long time before speaking.

"What's the matter, Danvel?" she asked intuitively. I was trying not to show any negative emotion but something had been gnawing at the back of my head.

"It's just that... I spent my whole life knowing that my parents were killed by a crazed Dragon in a random fight. That my father went out fighting to protect my family against something unpredictable. But all this time, the Dragons that I felt were the most honorable were the least. My father died because one evil Dragon wanted me out of the way. My mother died for the same reason. Gunther's parents, too. I don't really know how to feel about it. I don't really know that I can feel about it." She gave me a hug that seemed to last for a long time, but I knew it was just a moment.

"I don't think you should know how to feel about it, Danvel. We've all had our lives changed and ripped apart just in moments. Wyrmvale could be a barren wasteland at this point and Dragonia could suffer the same fate if Tiamat comes this way. We just have to take it one day at a time." She was right. I didn't have to know how I felt about it right now, or ever. I just needed to know the truth and let it become the truth for me. I smiled at her.

"I'm not going to be back for a while, you know?" I asked Gale.

"I know, but by the time you're back, I'll have the wedding planned," she said with a wink. We spent the rest of the day together before the adventure resumed.

Dragonia

Axdremaria

Morning

"So I believe that the statement was that you'd get us to Salamandra faster than a Wind Sprite farts... How fast is that?" I asked as we trudged along the Dragonia landscape. There hadn't been any rain the whole trip and the lakes seemed to be just where they should, not overflowing and creating mud I would get stuck in.

"Well... faster than walking all through the Desert of Rebirth, Wyrmvale, and most of the barren part of Salamandra. We'll ride a river along the Lakes of Astoria. Very secret and most

Dragons don't know about it. Leads right to the heartland of Salamandra," Hourig answered.

"Will we be able to get there if the Lakes of Astoria is flooded?" Murlan asked. "I thought that Leviathan had blocked all the ways to the Dragon Slayer Temple."

"Are you daft, Murlan? Or just too smart to use common sense? Leviathan is dead. So the one way that she blocked using her own powers should be clear. I mean look at everything around us! It's reverting back to its natural form. That Leviathan sure made a mess of the natural environment around here," Hourig commented.

"Always said that damn Dragon had too much power. Plus she was kind of a dick," I added.

"Totally," everyone agreed. Looking around, Hourig was definitely right. We were seeing animals we hadn't seen the first trip. Flowers were blooming everywhere. The whole environment seemed much more at peace. It was a good refreshing journey. I knew we wouldn't have many more of these after this so I tried to enjoy it as much as possible.

Time passed fast as we traveled and we had no interruptions. We didn't make many appearances in towns so that no one would know where we were. We didn't know how many Water Dragons had been loyal to Leviathan and if they had any way to communicate with Tiamat or his agents.

Then we reached the Lakes of Astoria, one of the few places in Dragonia I hadn't seen. It was absolutely beautiful. Lakes as far as the eye could see and crystal clear! Jeff jumped right into the nearest one and began swimming around. Hourig sat at the edge of the lake looking around.

"What is it?" I asked as I walked up beside him. Murlan and Aturdokht began walking along a path between lakes.

"Just seems like a good place for an ambush is all… or something." I looked around and agreed.

"Seems oddly still, but without Leviathan maybe that's the way it is." Even as I said it, the words didn't sit right in my mouth. "Jeff, come on out of the water until we know it's safe!"

"NEIGHHHH," Jeff replied, shaking his head no vehemently. I stamped my feet, which wasn't my best idea; my ribs still ached from time to time. I winced and stumbled a bit. Jeff came bounding out at that, though. Right as he jumped out, a large serpent like Dragon snapped at him. Jeff hightailed it away. Literally, his tail was very high in the air.

I pulled my sword, something I was getting increasingly more adept at and stood at the ready. Then a similar Dragon rose from each of the lakes. Then more than one rose from the lakes. There had to be hundreds of them. Aturdokht and Murlan both retreated to our location.

"What the heck are they?" Aturdokht asked. It was unusual to hear him talk. They looked at us curiously and didn't seem to harbor any malice towards us. Each of the Dragons had the same cerulean scales as Leviathan and many of the same features.

"I think they're Leviathan's children," I said in shock. "Do you think that's the reason she flooded the lakes? To protect her offspring?" They continued to watch us curiously. Then one of them moved forward, closer to us. Its scales had an extreme luster to them and the cerulean seemed to be much more intense than that of Leviathans. Then I noticed that it also had specks of silver scales as well. It must have been Tiamat's offspring as well.

"Ex...Excuse me, do you know where my mommy is?" it sputtered out. "She was supposed to come back to us after she completed her plan… but that was a while ago." An anger rose throughout me. Not at the young Dragon, but at Leviathan. How could she have left her children unattended just to go off and kill who knows how many?

Hourig started to speak but I stopped him. I'm sure it would have been something rude and awful. I thought it about it for a moment, put my head in my hands, and let out a long sigh. "Your mom… well… she didn't make it. We met her in Axdremaria when she enacted her plan." The baby Dragons all let out an awful shriek. The wailing continued for quite some time before they settled down. .

"What will we do now, human? We know very little of this world and without our mother to teach us. What will we do?" the lead one cried. The wailing began again.

"Enough," I yelled. "Your mother may have perished but that doesn't mean it's the end for you. Both of my parents were killed when I was a young age and I turned out relatively... okay...kind of. There are other people who can teach you and help you grow. Do you know the way to Axdremaria?" Hourig and the group looked at me in alarm but I raised my hand to stay their worry.

The lead Dragon cocked her head in thought. It turned back to its kin and began to converse in hushed tones. Hourig took the moment to come over and pull me aside. "Are you daft, boy? You can't send them to Axdremaria after what just happened! Are you trying to get them slaughtered?" I smacked Hourig right across the face in anger.

"How dare you accuse me of that? You know my history! Everyone does after Leviathan announced it in front of the whole damn town. And you know what I say? I'm sick of tired of Leviathan making orphans. If we want to repair the damage that she did with my parents, Gunther's parents, and her own kids, it starts here! With all of us banding together. We can't be Dragons and humanoids anymore. We have to be more than that. We have to be brothers and family. We have to truly take care of one another." Hourig quickly backed down. Probably one of the few times in his life that he did.

"You're right, Danvel. We need to be examples to the future generations so this doesn't happen again… Go on," he said, motioning to the on looking baby Leviathan's. The lead one had resumed her position as speaker.

"We do know the way to Axdremaria, but may I ask your name?" she said meekly.

"Only if you tell me yours. I'm Danvel," I replied with a short bow.

"I am Lendra... That wouldn't happen to be Danvel, the Dragon Slayer would it?" she asked with the same meek voice. I casually placed my hand on my sword and smiled at her. She didn't look like she was going to attack, but it was always good to be prepared.

"That would be something that some people call me," I replied simply. The Dragons responded by cowering towards the back of the lakes they were in.

"Please don't kill us, sir. Please," she pleaded in between sobbing. All of the others joined in the pleading making a chorus of blubbering and desperate cries.

"Wait a second," I tried to get in, but they weren't having it. Hourig stepped in front of me and puffed up, increasing his glow.

"Shut the hell up you sniveling brats! You make me disgusted to be a Dragon! Stand up straight and look presentable! Fafnir's beard, you all give Dragon's bad names, sniveling like that.

If Danvel were here to kill you, you'd all be dead! And if he just randomly killed Dragons, what the heck are my son and I doing here?" he said flailing his arms around to bring his point home. "Listen to what he has to say. He hasn't guided me wrong yet!" He went back to his place beside me and I moved forward again.

"First time for everything," I mumbled under my breath. "Thanks for the pseudo pep talk, Hourig. So here's the deal. Axdremaria just suffered a catastrophic event. We need someone to help defend it in case of attack. Go there and help. Work with the humanoids there and learn about the world. There will be a Water Dragon, Lynnaedra, who can help you learn and the Human leader will help, too. Just tell them that Danvel sent you and tell them you're orphans. They'll take care of you." Lendra went back to her siblings and conversed with them.

We waited around awkwardly until they finished their conversation. Eventually Lendra popped back over. "We think that your plan makes a lot of sense. We want to do something good in this world and make our mother proud of us!" I felt guilty for not telling them more about their mother, but I thought it was best not to change their mind from the goodness they sought.

"Then it's settled! Off you go to start something good! Take care of the people there, please," I said as a goodbye. The hundreds of baby Leviathans exited their lakes and made way towards the sea. It was good to know that something positive would come from Leviathan's dark deeds.

"So where's this secret river then, Hourig?" I asked as I started to walk in between the lakes. Hourig ran to catch up with me and the others followed behind. The lakes continued on and on for as far as the eye could see, but there was no river in plain sight.

"Well it's hidden, or else everyone would know about it," Hourig replied with a wink. He dashed on past me and led us further into the lakes. Soon the pathways were becoming thinner and eventually they stopped revealing a massive lake in front of us. It almost looked like an ocean! "This is the Great Lake of Astoria and the biggest lake on Draco," he announced.

"That's awesome and all, but still not seeing any river," I exclaimed. Hourig slapped me on the back, nearly knocking me into the lake. Jeff caught me before I fell in. My ribs ached again so I gave him a smack back.

"Just wait for it, boy," he said with more patience than I thought it possible for him to convey. We waited just like he asked. I sat with my feet in the lake (yes, I removed pieces of my armor). Jeff swam again, but closer this time, not daring to go out very far. Murlan was talking about something to Aturdokht and Hourig I swear was asleep.

I gazed up into the lake and noticed what I would call a bulge coming towards us in the water. It didn't look like anything more than a wave, but my recent experiences told me that looks could be deceiving. I smacked Hourig waking him up. "Something's coming our way, olden."

Hourig hopped to and rose on his hind legs. He looked taller than I thought he would. Jeff jumped out of the lake and sat beside me. I had already pulled on my armor and Murlan and Aturdokht stood at attention. The bulge got closer and eventually stopped about ten feet in front of us.

The bulge increased in size, rising from the water. Then it broke the surface, revealing a type of long-necked animal with a massive hump. It wasn't quite a Dragon but wasn't quite anything else either. I couldn't even really describe its color as it seemed to flow through different ones. "River, it is great to see you," Hourig called. Of course its name is river.

"As it is to see you, Hourig. You have a great host with you today. I assume you seek transport to Salamandra?" River asked gently. It was truly a massive creature and could easily hold all of us on its hump.

"You assume correctly, River. Salamandra is in grave danger and we have to get there soon to warn everyone. War has broken out between the Dragons, but Fafnir and the Salamanders may be unprepared. We need your greatest pace," Hourig implored.

"You know I would take you to Salamandra as fast as possible but it seems I cannot take you very far. The river that leads into Salamandra has frozen over right at the border. It is completely unwarranted. Some force has to be there, freezing it constantly. Nothing less could halt the heat of Salamandra," River explained. We boarded River, something that went much more smoothly than I would have suspected. It's hump was soft yet didn't yield easily to our weight. It wasn't slippery like I expected and only Jeff had trouble keeping his footing while getting on.

"Hold on tight, everyone," River announced. Then he started moving... fast. Faster than I expected the cumbersome beast was able to. Soon the land we were just on was no longer visible. We barely talked as we rode and only I had the stomach to eat. Jeff and Hourig slept while Murlan and Aturdokht continued their ongoing conversation.

Night came on fast and the stars began decorating the sky. "I think it's best if we stop for the night," River called back to us. She moved us to shore and dropped us off. "I will be back at sunrise. Be wary, we are near the border so Ice Dragons may be patrolling near here. River sunk back into the lake, leaving us all alone. Hourig and Aturdokht turned up their glow illuminating everything around them.

"So who else hates riding on a sea monster thing all day?" I asked to no one in particular. Everyone agreed and moved off of the shore further into wherever we were. I assumed it was Wyrmvale, but without any light there was no way of confirming it. We reached an area that seemed easily defendable and sat down. It was good being on dry, stable land. I was beginning to hate water. First, with the Leviathan fight and now this. Hourig opted to take the first watch as he got the most sleep on the journey here. We soon drifted off to a sound sleep.

Chapter 13 - Out of the Frying Pan and into the Lava

Near The Border to Salamandra

Sunrise

The morning sun was pleasant feeling as I started to wake up. I didn't enjoy the freezing breeze that seemed to blow by every few minutes, however. I looked around noting that everyone was present and accounted for. Hourig was looking off towards the east. "What do you see, olden?" I asked as I stood up.

"That cold wind is coming from the direction of Salamandra. We have to be getting close to the source of the ice, then. Or sources I suppose. It would take a great amount of ice to do this." Hourig had a small look of worry on his face and I suppose I understood it. If Salamandra's border was already overtaken by invaders, who knows if there would be anyone left to warn and help defend.

"Don't worry. We'll stop them," I said as I put my hand on his shoulder. "Do we hoof it, or head back to find River?" I looked around at everyone rousing and getting their packs ready. Jeff was already at his feet and had both of our packs ready to go. Jeff never did like the cold. He hated it in Asgard.

"I already sent River ahead to see if the ice is spreading so we'll be going by foot. It isn't that far… maybe a mile or two? Shouldn't take too long at all," Hourig assured us. It took us six hours of walking to see the first bits of ice. The air was becoming more chilled and the wind was fierce. Murlan had to put his hat in his pack so it didn't blow away.

Then it started to snow. At first it was flurries but each step we took it got worse until we were in white out conditions. We each had a hand on the other so we didn't lose on another but it was slow moving. "Whatever is up ahead has to be pretty freaking strong to cause a blizzard like this," I yelled above the roaring wind. Hourig didn't answer but I was sure he was thinking the same thing.

We pushed on until Hourig stopped. I slammed right into him which ended up causing a small train wreck. As I picked myself and Jeff off of the ground Hourig took in a deep breath and spit out some fire in front of us. I could see two bodies run off and the blizzard let up some.

"It's a Drake and an Ice Dragon. They're using his wind to amplify the cold," Hourig yelled. He began shooting out random spots of fire while I grabbed my sword and looked around. The blizzard kept increasing and decreasing in intensity as Hourig shot at them.

Aturdokht joined in, shooting in the opposite direction of Hourig. I kept my eyes on the fire, hoping to catch a glimpse. The blizzard intensity increased exponentially after a while and soon it was nearly impossible to move. That's when I realized we were thinking about the battle in the wrong manner. Drakes can fly!

"Aturdokht! Shoot a spread up in the sky! Hourig! Throw me," I yelled. Hourig obliged and threw me straight up. I looked around and saw that the Drake was in the air and that he was holding the Ice Dragon. I plowed into the snow right beside Jeff who was laying underneath Aturdokht for warmth. Murlan pulled me up out of the snow.

"What did you see?" he asked as I brushed the snow off of me. I ignored his question and ran over to Hourig. I pulled my pack from the snow and ripped Gunther's bow from it. I pulled an arrow from the pack and shot an arrow straight up in the air. I sent another arrow up after it and it was followed by two thuds. The blizzard mostly cleared up and I put the bow back in my pack.

"I saw two dead Dragons," I said answering Murlan. "This can't be what's causing the freeze though. No way two puny Dragons were able to cause this much cold. Plus it's still snowing," I said as I examined the bodies. The Ice Dragon's skin was as white as the snow around it. It was an almost perfect camouflage.

He was hard to the touch and cold, like his scales were made out of pure ice. I stabbed my sword into them again just to make sure. As certain as I was that they were dead, I liked to make sure with my sword. Hourig walked over and inspected them with me.

"I've never seen an Ice Dragon before. Doesn't look like much," he said with a snort. I thought they looked just like a Fire Dragon but I didn't say anything. I imagine there would have been a blue glow like Hourig's fire glow. I pulled the arrow out of them, replaced them in the pack and went over to the rest of the group.

"How far from the border are we, do you think?" I asked Aturdokht. I didn't trust Hourig's sense of distance anymore. Plus he was more interested in mocking the dead corpse instead of deciding our next move. Jeff and Murlan were shivering and wrapping blankets from my pack around them.

"I'd say maybe two miles, but it's hard to really tell with all of this snow everywhere. I think we should go this way," he said pointing to the south east. "That way we can reach the river and the border at around the same time."

"Sounds like a plan." I grabbed my pack and got ready to travel again. "Hourig, stop playing with the enemy and get over here!" Hourig listened and trotted over to join us. I ran ahead of the group to try and do some scouting but quickly found myself stuck in two and a half feet of snow. I raised my arms up until someone caught up and pulled me out. Hourig chuckled.

"Just like the mud back in Dragonia, young Danvel." I wasn't happy about it, but he was right. I hated getting stuck. He placed me on his back and we both went ahead of the group to scout. We reached the river in ten minutes but it was hard to see anything. Steam rose from everywhere and whatever you could see was blurred from the snow flurry.

"I think we're here," I announced. I stepped out onto the river to see how thick the ice was. It supported me fine, but I was worried that Hourig's heat would melt it and cause us all to fall in. "What kind of creature do you think would be able to do this?" Hourig shook his head.

"Nothing I know about. Obviously not the Ice Dragon we saw or anything like it," Hourig said, thinking over his lore. The ice cracked very loudly causing Hourig to jump back in surprise. I laughed at him.

"For all your knowledge you don't know that when ice cracks it's usually just because the ice is expanding! Such a funny Dragon." That was when the tentacles burst out of the ice and pulled me under. To say that the water was cold was about the dumbest statement I could think of. It was freaking freezing. I reached for my sword to find that it was already beginning to freeze to my armor.

I grabbed the tentacles and squeezed as hard as I could (which wasn't very hard since my gloves seemed to be frozen as well). I looked in front of me to see a squid like monster. A Kraken… An Ice Kraken. I heard a muffled noise and saw that Hourig and Aturdokht had appeared beside me and were generating lots of heat.

I grabbed for my sword again and thankfully it was able to be freed. I sliced the tentacles off of me and neared the two Dragons for warmth. I felt like I was about to fall asleep. We moved forward in unison, not something that's easy when you have two Dragons who weren't used to the water and a half frozen Dragon Slayer.

The Kraken was reeling in pain, but quickly recovered and focused its attention on us. The ice above began to expand downward slowly and it moved its tentacles below us to trap us in between. Aturdokht dove upward and let loose with shots of fire. I started hacking at the tentacles (there were hundreds of them), to buy us some time. This left Hourig to deal with the actual beast.

Hourig dove right at it, slamming into it with a large amount of force. This stunned it momentarily, but only made it angrier. The Kraken pulled the tentacles away from me, not that I had done much damage, and wrapped them around Hourig and Aturdokht. I assume that he did not like heat. I charged at him as I saw the two Dragons push more heat from their body and sear the tentacles.

I stabbed my sword right above his beak and between his two huge eyes. The creature tried to pull back but I pressed hard until the hilt of the sword was the only thing that could be seen. It let go of Hourig and Aturdokht, but still the ice continued to grow. Apparently this thing had a bigger brain than I would give it credit for and I was running out of air! I ripped the sword from his head and began to stab in and out furiously. The ice continued to grow.

At this point half of the river was frozen above us and I probably wouldn't have lasted much longer. Then River showed up and pushed something over my mouth and nose. It was disgusting and wriggled its way through my mouth and down into my lungs, filling them up with air. I turned around to see Hourig and Aturdokht unleashing fire blasts onto the Kraken and it becoming more and more dead. The ice stopped spreading and we all breathed (or whatever I was doing exactly) a sigh of relief. In fact, the ice started to recede.

River burst up through the ice and let us all out of the water. I ripped the thing off of my face (which was much worse than I thought it would have been) and breathed non-aided air. Then I threw up. After I recovered I looked around to see that the snow and wind had stopped. The steam was still pouring out from the ground and the river.

"What the hell was that, River?" I exclaimed. My mouth tasted like fish, and not the good kind. I was still spitting and rinsing my mouth out with ice water. The thing in my mouth scuttled off and dove back into the river.

"That was a Snorkelfish. Breathes air into humanoids and Dragons who are about to drown. Good creatures." Hourig and Aturdokht lay on the ground breathing heavily. Murlan and Jeff just ran over from where they were. Apparently we had moved down the river a considerable amount.

It didn't take long for all the snow and ice to have melted. I was glad to feel some of the warmth seep into my bones. "I think, that I'm done for the day," I announced. My muscles didn't want to move much and I could tell that Hourig and Aturdokht were in agreeance.

We set up camp and laid down. By the time my head hit the pillow I could already hear Jeff snoring. "Lightweight," I started to mumble, but fell asleep before finishing.

Right at the Border of Salamandra

Noon

It didn't take long for the raging heat to wake us up. Maybe it was because we had just gotten accustomed to the cold, but I was burning up! Murlan and Jeff, too!

"Neighhhh," Jeff pouted as he kicked off his armor and put it in his pack. I had a mind to do the same thing, but didn't bring my summer armor.

"I miss the Ice Kraken," I announced. Jeff and Murlan agreed. Hourig and Aturdokht were enjoying the heat. Freaking Fire Dragons. Salamandra's heat was caused by nearly thirty active volcanoes that were spread across the country. There was at least one eruption per day on each volcano and lava flowed in rivers.

Traversing it wasn't hard as terrain would go. Salamandra was mostly flat except for the volcanoes and geysers. Not many people dared cross it by foot but it was the fastest way to reach it since Leviathan wasn't manipulating the water to speed things along. Not even the Fire Dragons tread it regularly.

"We'll have to hurry across the plains. An eruption near here could flood them with lava very quickly. We'll head to Mount Agnor. It's the nearest high ground and will keep us safe for a while." We started at a good pace. Hourig at the front and Aturdokht bringing up the rear. I ran in the middle to make sure Murlan could keep pace.

The heat slowly began increasing as we went further in. I ripped off my helmet and threw it in my pack. The ground began to shake, toppling Murlan but leaving the rest on our feet. "That's the first eruption of the day," Hourig called. "The rest of the volcanoes will begin to erupt soon and flood right where we're standing! We have to move faster!" We doubled our speed.

The second and third eruption happened soon after. The heat began to rise even faster and in the distance the air started to warp from the heat. Not far behind that would be the lava and Mount Agnor wasn't in sight yet. Murlan tripped so I picked him up and threw him over Jeff's back. Jeff started to object, turning back to yell at me, but then he saw what was behind us and galloped forward.

Fourth and fifth eruption. The lava was now in sight behind us and Mount Agnor finally came into view. The heat was getting unbearable and Jeff and I had to take two breaks to get some water in our systems. We continued at a rough pace, the lava getting closer and closer.

Six and seventh eruption. The air was becoming hard to breathe but Mount Agnor was fully in our sight. Hourig and Aturdokht pushed at a terrible pace, but we knew we had to keep up. Jeff fell over from exhaustion and Hourig took him and Aturdokht picked up Murlan.

Eighth and ninth eruption. We scrambled up the mountain as the lava poured into its base. We barely escaped in time but luckily we had gotten far enough up it that we were safe. Hourig and

Aturdokht led us to a cave that was relatively cool and we rested for a long time.

"How long til the lava will recede?" I asked pulling my armor off. I reached into my pack and pulled out what was left of my water and chugged it. I pulled out Murlan and Jeff's and gave some to both of them. Jeff perked up right away and drank away, but Murlan took a little more coaxing.

"It really depends on the rest of the eruptions. We felt around ten, so hopefully that was the close volcanoes. It usually drains out in about an hour. The good news is we made it a good distance into Salamandra. We're less than a day's travel from Hellbender. Fafnir, and hopefully James, will be there." Aturdokht stayed at the cave entrance while the rest of us stretched and got ready for the next leg of this gauntlet.

Mount Agnor was like an oasis in a desert. One of the few spots that offered refuge against the harsh conditions. Salamandra had a few of them across the country, but not enough to let travel be a commonplace thing. I went back farther into the cave to breathe in the cool air. It was nice to feel the chill breeze without my armor.

Murlan was finally getting up and moving around. Jeff was putting his armor back on and I joined him. I stepped outside with Aturdokht and took it all in. Lava as far as the eye could see. This continent seemed to be full of amazing and frightening sights. I climbed to the top of the mountain (we were about halfway up) and looked out in the direction we needed to go. There was smoke rising in the distance which could be a bad thing but I've never been to Hellbender so maybe it was the norm there.

"Truly marvelous," Aturdokht said from behind me. "Traveling so much doesn't afford me the time to truly appreciate the beauty of my home."

"I never really called any place home after my parents were killed. Well... murdered. Never stayed in one place long enough. Always on the move. Looking for something to do if a quest didn't find me. But I tell you after this... I wouldn't mind calling a place my home and settling down. Get myself away from the excitement for a while." Aturdokht looked stunned after I said that.

"You're starting to sound like an old man," Hourig called from behind us.

"Neighhhh," Jeff mocked as he exited the cave.

"Coming from the Sleipnir who can't even handle a little heat," I struck back. "You're just mad because you haven't done any killing lately."

"Neigh neigh neigh neigh neigh neigh neigh,' Jeff said with a sneer.

"It's not my fault that the Ice Kraken pulled me under the ice! I'm sure that it didn't look up above the ice and think, 'hmmm, I have a choice between two Dragons, two humans, and a Sleipnir. I'm going to choose the small Human.' That's not how it works. Plus, you didn't have that disgusting Snorkelfish shoved down your throat!" Jeff stuck his tongue out at me so I threw a rock at him.

"Quit it, you two. We don't need anyone getting knocked into the lava," Hourig barked. I threw a rock at him. He huffed and went back to the bottom of the mountain. The lava had begun receding leaving seared dirt beneath it. We followed him down to the base. The air was still a little hot to breathe in but we could start on the road again!

"Let's get to Hellbender!" We marched along towards the capital city.

Salamandra

Outside of Hellbender

Sunset

Hellbender was surprisingly nice. I expected a half run down town, worn down by the heat; it was quite the opposite. It was magnificent. It had architecture like I had never seen before. The rooftops were flat since there was no natural rain. The houses shone bright red and yellow, matching the flame theme of their country. Also there was a fire castle.

It shone bright red, yellow, and blue; flickering between these three colors. It cast a great light into the darkness of the sunset. We moved through the town silently and headed straight for the castle. The town was relatively quiet and it was obvious that no battle had taken place... yet.

Soon we reached the castle perimeter. They had a moat of lava! A pride of Lionmen guarded the entrance and surrounded us as we approach. "Halt! Who goes there?" the leader of their pride called. He was easily the largest Lionman I had ever seen. He was double my height and immense. He could easily rend a normal human's body in half.

"I am Danvel, the Dragon Slayer and this is my company. Hourig and his son Aturdokht, Fire Dragons (I mentioned them first in hopes to set the Lionmen at ease), Jeff the Sleipnir, and Murlan the Wizard. We came seeking an audience with Fafnir and the King of the Lion Pride. We have grave news of happenings from the other countries. Also, if you've come across news of James the Earthwyrm, I would much appreciate it," I explained.

The Lionman regarded me for a long moment, said nothing, and jumped across the moat in one graceful leap. We were all duly impressed. He entered the castle and within a few awkward moments of being surrounded, returned. "You may enter, slayer. You and Hourig. The rest will receive housing in the nearby inn, the Mudpuppy. You two, come with me now! The rest go with the rest of the pride." He jumped back over the moat and began lowering the drawbridge.

"Winning personality," I said to Hourig. "Is it like a requirement for guards to be devoid of spunk?" The pride led the rest of the company away just as the drawbridge finished lowering. I gave Jeff a high five so he knew that when I mentioned the names of everyone else to the Lionman that he came first in my mind. He gets jealous about these things.

We crossed the drawbridge and saw that we were being watched by keen eyes. There were Lionmen in each tower and I assume more eyes on us than we could actually see. The castle was very well protected which boded well for the coming battle.

Inside the castle walls there were several Salamanders and Fire Dragons in intensive training. What's the difference you ask? Salamanders were shorter than the Dragons and had longer tails. They were also more in tune with the element of fire than the Dragons. While Hourig and Aturdokht couldn't have survived direct contact with lava, Salamanders were born inside it and spent a large part of their childhood there as well.

Inside the castle was amazing, too. Fire was used as a decoration (which seems superbly dangerous but awesome). It crawled up the walls in a rhythmic fashion which if stared at long enough surely would cause some type of hypnosis. The Lionman left me no time to admire it though as we were already entering the throne room. It was larger than all of the other throne rooms I had seen, full of a collection of people.

"I present Danvel the Dragon Slayer and Hourig the Old," the Lionman announced. Hourig grumbled something under his breath about not being too old, but he knew it was a term of endearment. A Lionman even more massive than the one who brought us here stood up out of his throne. He looked like if a Norse god had been mixed with a lion. His mane made my beard look like a baby Dwarves.

"Come, come," he called with much mirth. He motioned us towards him and caused the host of people to part for us. There were Lionmen, Salamanders, Dwarves and Wyrms. Hopefully that meant that James had made it here safely. "My name is Ariel, and welcome to my Kingdom, Slayer... Hourig," he said with a slight scowl. I detected a little tension between them. "What brings you hear, Danvel. James told me you had been sent off to Leviathan to warn her about the impending threat of Tiamat. And I'm surprised to see that Hourig the great traveling ancient would be kind enough to actually return to his home, despite my many requests for his council in my court."

Hourig didn't reply and I don't expect he wanted anyone to hear what he had to say anyways. "Well it seems that Leviathan was in on the whole plan with Tiamat, sir. She killed nearly all the knights in the castle and killed Baron Dexter," I explained.

Ariel looked shocked at this. "Dexter dead? It is an awful thing. Dexter was a dear friend and so was his host. Where has that evil serpent slithered off to now?" Ariel slammed his fist down on the armrest of this throne.

"Nowhere, sir. Leviathan is dead. I killed her," I said in a serious tone. The crowd gasped in shock. I guess it wasn't every day that a Patron Dragon was slain. "It wasn't without casualties, however. She struck Axdremaria with two massive tidal waves, killing many and leaving the rest without homes. If I hadn't stopped her, I imagine all of Dragonia would be devoid of humanoids."

"This is truly grave news," Ariel replied. "We must let James and Fafnir know immediately! Send relief to Axdremaria as fast as possible," he said as he started to walk way. I grabbed him and stopped him which provoked the guards to jump towards me.

"I'm not finished, Ariel," I spat out putting my hand on my sword. Hourig moved himself between me and the Lionmen guards.

"Leviathan bragged about how she had sent a legion of Ice Dragons against the forces of Salamandra. We ran across some ice creatures on the southern border to Salamandra. You have to prepare for war." Ariel shrugged me off and snorted at me.

"No one can make it through the lava fields, Danvel. Hellbender is the safest place on the continent. We are guarded by sea and have the best natural defenses of any country." He left the room and disappeared.

I turned to Hourig and pointed to the door. "We're leaving!" The guards tried to block the door but we physically suggested that they should move out of the way. They obliged. We ran down and out of the castle to see the King just making it across the drawbridge. As soon as he stepped off, it started to rise. We ran to the Lionmen who were raising it and suggested that they lower it back down. They obliged as well. By the time we had crossed the drawbridge, the King was barely in sight. We ran after him as fast as we could but he moved so fast!

I looked behind us to see the King's guard chasing after us and gaining. Gaining until they suddenly became kitten like. Jeff and Murlan we're on the edge of town, chasing after us and Aturdokht was behind them keeping some more Lionmen at bay. Dwarves had joined the fray and were blocking the Lionmen as well. Apparently they felt that what I had to say was worth listening to.

The King was still moving out of sight until Jeff came up behind me and moved his head down in between my legs. I stopped and was easily scooped up into his gait. He launched himself forward, chasing down the King at full speed. Normally a horse couldn't catch up with a Lionman, but Sleipnirs boasted massive speed (perfect for the Norse to plow down their enemies).

We had him in good sights and saw that he was heading towards a massive mountain in the distance. We kept our distance so we didn't alert him to our presence. Eventually he closed in on a cave on the side of the mountain that was guarded by a large pride of Lionmen. He entered leaving Jeff and me to deal with them.

As soon as we entered their line of sight, they charged after us at full speed. I felt like this gave me a total advantage. As they leapt at us, I stuck my fists out striking one clean in the face and knocking it down. The other tackled me, knocking me back several feet. Jeff had jumped above his attackers and struck one with his full weight, knocking it out. This left six more to deal with.

I drove up from the ground, tackling the one who tackled me. One good strike to the head put him down and I was off to the next target. It didn't take long to wrap the fight up. Jeff and I looked unscathed, but as soon as Jeff took me in, he started laughing hysterically.

I looked down and saw that the bastard's claws had sheared off a chunk of my beard! I was pissed. I charged into the cave where the King was conversing with Fafnir and James and several other smaller Dragons, Wyrms, and Salamanders. I interrupted his speech with a knock to the head, rendering him unconscious.

"That's for my beard, dick," I yelled. He did not hear me. The Dragons all looked at me stunned. "His Lionmen cut my beard. He's lucky I didn't kill anyone," I explained. Surprisingly they all just accepted this explanation. James stepped forward (and over the King) to greet us.

"Danvel, it is great to see you again," he belted out. "Ariel here was trying to tell us something you said before... you knocked him out." He nudged the King a little but he was out cold. "Where are my manners?" he said as he motioned over to Fafnir. At least I assumed it was Fafnir by the fact that he was larger than all the other

Dragons in the vicinity. "This is Fafnir. The great Patron Dragon of Salamandra."

All of the Dragons bowed. Jeff and I, of course, did not. "Pleased to meet you," he said in a wispy voice. He looked similar to James but he wore a massive beard that traveled down his belly and the whole length of his tail. "I've heard great things about your deeds! Please inform us what you came to say!" I filled them in about the attack of Leviathan and her bragging about the legion of Ice Dragons. Then I filled them in about King Moron.

"Salamanders, prepare the city for battle! Tell the Lionmen to fall in line or be imprisoned in the castle! Give Danvel and his men whatever they need. They're going to be helping wage this battle," Fafnir cried out. At about the same time, Hourig, Aturdokht, Murlan, and several Dwarves came bursting in. I leapt in front of them.

"Meet my posse," I said coolly. Fafnir came barreling over.

"Hourig! It is great to see you, old friend. I heard you were traveling the world again so I should have figured you'd get mixed up in this kind of thing. Keeping everyone in line I hope," Fafnir gave him a quick punch on the shoulder, nearly knocking Hourig off his feet. Hourig stood up and knocked Fafnir over with a great tackle.

"Still spry enough to knock you on your ass, oh great patron," he said mockingly. It was interesting to see that Hourig was held in such high esteem with Fafnir, but such contempt with the King of the Pride. The Fire Dragons and Salamanders moved out to follow Fafnir's orders. As Hourig and Fafnir reminisced, James made his way over to Jeff, Gunther, and me.

"Danvel, I have some surprising news to share with you. Follow me," he said as he waved us to follow. He led us outside this cave and around the mountain to a well-hidden cave. I assumed that this was perhaps his quarters for now. We entered to a dimly lit room with a bed in the middle. In the bed lay Gunther, his hand still gripped tightly around Muramasa.

"Oh my gosh! Gunther! Where did you find him?" I asked as I rushed over to his side. He had dark bags under his eyes and gave off an intermittent dark glow that was seemed to be a sign of dark magic.

"When my Wyrms returned to see how Heartha had fared against Tiamat's winds, we found that he was the only thing left. All the buildings had been stripped away, but Gunther lay in the middle of the town, completely unscathed. He hasn't woken up since then. I imagine that his pure soul is warring against the darkness that is Muramasa.

"Well if he's still alive, that just means we have to fight harder to win this battle then. We're going to save him, just like he saved us!"

Chapter 14 - Two if by Sea

Salamandra

Mudpuppy Inn

Midday

The anticipation of battle was nerve racking. We had been waiting for a week for these Ice Dragons to show up but there had been no sign of them yet. Every scout we sent back into the lava plains came back with the same response. Nothing to report. I had started to feel like the King had a point about nobody being able to pass through the lava plains (except us, that is). We had all types of patrols constantly going around the perimeter day and night. I wasn't happy about our numbers for the battle, either. James and Fafnir had the majority of their forces in Wyrmvale in search and rescue operations.

I had just drank a rather tall glass of mead and sat back in my chair. "It makes no sense! Why would Leviathan brag about something that wasn't going to happen? Mind games? That seems beyond her capabilities and doesn't make sense if she expected me to die."

"Neeighhhhh," Jeff agreed as he took in a large glass of mead himself. We all were getting stir crazy. Murlan had spent his time trying to reverse the kittens that he made earlier to no avail and Hourig and Aturdokht were out leading patrols on a regular basis. I originally marched with them but soon realized it was unnecessary.

"I'm going for a walk to the beach, Jeff. No one to bother me there!" I left Jeff to his mead and dashed out of the inn. The shore wasn't too far away from the inn and the patrols were mostly ignoring it since Leviathan had died. It was a great place for peace and quiet. When I reached it there were only two Lionmen watching the docks and ships. Shipments had stopped except to send relief to Axdremaria. No ships had come in at all.

I walked along thinking over everything that had happened with Leviathan to make sure I didn't miss anything. Eventually I reached the docks where the two Lionmen were standing. They didn't say anything to me but the one shivered for a moment. I gave him a strange look.

"What's the matter, slayer?" he said with a slight disdain. "Haven't you ever seen anyone get cold before?" He scoffed and turned around.

"No, not in Salamandra," I said as I took off my helmet. A cold breeze came across my face and then I finally understood. We were about to get massacred. "Go get every patrol right now," I screamed at them while I pulled my sword. "The bastards aren't coming through the lava plains! They're freezing the oceans and walking over on it!" The Lionmen turned towards the sea and focused their eyes.

"By Fafnir's beard, there are thousands of them!" The Lionmen dashed off in different directions leaving me to wait for destruction. It took a few moments for them to come into view, but when they did, it was an awful sight. Two massive Ice Dragons stood in front, breathing ice breath into the ocean. In front of them, you could see two tentacles leading them forward. Another Ice Kraken.

Jeff and Murlan raced up behind me. "We heard a commotion but… oh my stars and garters,' Murlan exclaimed.

"Neigh…," Jeff said in awe.

"Any suggestions?" I asked not expecting any answer. I didn't receive one. The Ice Dragons had nearly reached the shore when the Ice Kraken came bursting up out of the water and beached itself in front of them. It spat out ice at us and we dodged as best we could. I launched myself at it, but its tentacles just swatted me away.

I looked up to see fireballs flying and hitting the Kraken, but doing no significant damage. I retreated back to Jeff and Murlan. "Murlan, we need to get rid of that thing!" I yelled. Another volley came in from the approaching patrols of Fire Dragons and Salamanders but the results were the same.

"What do you expect me to do about it?" he yelled. I slapped him across the face semi hard.

"Get angry!" Murlan began to glow like he did with the Chaos Snakelet and approached the Kraken. He raised his staff in the air and slammed it in the sand and then the Ice Kraken was gone. Murlan came back over, his nose bleeding and out of breath.

"There! He's gone," he said exasperated. We joined the incoming troops that we're holding their ground just on the edge of the beach. Fafnir, James, Hourig, and Aturdokht all came running up from a different direction.

"We got it all wrong," I yelled to them. The Ice Dragons moved the two unusually large ones back to the front and they began freezing whatever sea was left between them and the beach. "Hourig, I need a lift," I said softly. He obliged and launched me over to the Ice Dragons. I came down, driving my sword clean through the first massive Ice Dragon, ripped it out and sliced off the head of the other. The other Ice Dragons were about to overtake me but a well-timed volley pushed them off long enough for me to jump in the water and swim back to shore.

The other Ice Dragons took off where the other two left, but it was clear that their process would take much longer. The fire creatures and ice creatures began spitting rounds back and forth. James began hurling large chunks of rock that we expected would shatter their ice, but to our surprise most of the time it just landed on it. The Earthwyrms joined in on this tactic, but aiming their rocks at the now forming ice rather than the ice deeper in the sea.

"Humanoids retreat," I called. The humanoids listened and we all ran back to the city. The Dwarves retrieved their bows and I helped the Lionmen pull the catapults to the other side of the city. Before returning to the battle, I went to the Inn and retrieved Gunther's bow. The Dwarves had already formed a line and were preparing their arrows. I handed the bow to Murlan and didn't say any words, he knew what to do. By the time I reached the front of the line, the catapults were loaded and the Dwarves were ready.

"Everybody fire!!!" They let loose in a volley that felled many Ice Dragons, but their numbers were still so vast. Still over a thousand. Eventually they reached the beach. We started for it, but James called out, "hold your place everyone!" We listened and as the Ice Dragons came barreling down onto the beach, their gaits were stopped suddenly. They couldn't move their feet. The sand had become quicksand (James' doing of course). They quickly sank and whatever Ice Dragons got through were quickly mowed down by the Dragons on our line.

The Ice Dragons eventually stopped coming out and started to freeze ice over the beach and returned to sending ice volleys at us. We were doing well. Minimal losses and we had slowed the Ice Dragons progress. We could really do this! By the time they had frozen over the shore and reached our line, they were less than five hundred. The Dragons joined them in battle and we were charging to help when we heard a small voice call, "There is another battalion coming from the south shore!" We turned to see exactly what he described. A second battalion with nearly the same numbers as before, but this time there were Drakes with them.

We must have run into their scouts at the border. They had no Kraken with them so it was a safe bet to say it was them. "Humanoids, to the south shore!" We charged with weapons out to meet them. They were just pouring onto the beach when got there. Jeff, the Lionmen, and I jumped headfirst into the battle while the Dwarves and Murlan whittled down the back half of their troop.

The Drakes swooped over us and descended to attack our back half in response. We were pinned between two forces and with no hope of winning. I was swinging with wide arcs, hitting whatever piece of Dragon I could see. The Ice Dragons backed up and made a circle around us. They inhaled deep breaths, about to unleash their ice upon when Fafnir slammed down through them and broke through the ice. All the Ice Dragons on one side fell through. We charged the other side and pushed them back onto the shore.

James was going wild on the Drakes. His fury was something to behold, and even though he was flailing wildly about, he gracefully missed every single Dwarf. We cut down the Ice Dragon's between us and the Dwarves and pulled them out from the fray. We retreated to the city with our Dragons following tightly behind. James had disposed of many Drakes and the rest retreated with the Ice Dragons. Fafnir and James then met with us in the town.

The remaining Ice Dragons were repairing the damaged ice bridge and were making their way back to shore. There was still about a thousand left. It didn't take long until they were back on land and marching towards the city. James and Fafnir were ready for them, though. James placed his hand on the ground and closed his eyes in focus and Fafnir joined him. As the Ice Dragons came closer to the city, they found that some places in the ground simply fell out from beneath them and they were met with lava.

Murlan led whatever Dwarves were left to the rooftops and then began launching volleys at the Wind Drakes. Their numbers were beginning to dwindle but the Patron Dragons couldn't maintain the pitfalls for long (their powers weren't meant to be used in such a manner) and they rose from their focus. I was the first to meet the oncoming menace in battle again. I struck down nearly ten as they charged past me towards the city. The few that stopped to try and face me met the wrath of Jeff who was just behind me.

The rest ran past and started to ransack the city. The Lionmen fought hard to stop their homes from being destroyed, but in the end we knew that their numbers were too much. We had sent most of the population away to nearby mountains and were left with only a thousand Humanoids and Dragons to face the multitude of Dragons that had come to face us. All in all, I thought we were doing pretty well.

Jeff and I rushed back towards the city and attacked the Ice Dragons at the rear. Seeing how overrun the city was, I knew it was a losing fight. The Lionmen couldn't really hold their own one on one versus a Dragon (despite what they bragged) and the Dwarves were too little in number to hold off the Drakes. Our minimal Dragon battalion was being overwhelmed by their numbers. Hourig apparently had the same thoughts as he yelled for retreat from somewhere inside the city. A wall of flames burst up cutting the city in two and cutting the enemy off from our retreating forces.

I sent Jeff on ahead to the castle to ensure that no enemies would make it inside. I saw Fafnir carrying Aturdokht away in what looked like a struggle so I rushed into the city to find Hourig near the middle with an ice spear through his body. The flames burst up higher and then made a square around the Ice Dragons. The flames rose up high enough where even the Drakes were having trouble exiting the square.

I rushed over to Hourig. "Not looking your best, old man," I said as I inspected the wound. The ice spears were apparently meant to expand when they had found their mark and there was no getting it out.

"Sorry... sorry I couldn't look... more... dashing for you," he said struggling to get the words out. "You... you take care of

Aturdokht for me. He... he needs someone... fierce... like you to guide him. And... you take care of... yourself. You were like... a brother, Danvel. You... brought me back home." I was about to speak when he picked me up and threw me farther than I thought he could. I looked back to the city as it started to burst into flames. Then an eruption engulfed the whole thing.

Salamandra

Hellbender Castle

Night

"Where is Tiamat at?" I yelled as I slammed my sword through a nearby table. The Drake eyed my sword up and swallowed nervously. This Drake was the only survivor of Hourig's sacrifice. Somehow he got out of the flame square but his wings were damaged by the blast. Out of our thousand strong battle force only two hundred or so survived.

"Well... he's uhhh, he's up north that's for sure," he said trying to tiptoe around the question. I threw a piece of the broken table at him. I wasn't very happy. "He's far up north! At the tip of the continent. In Hyperborea," he said as I neared closer, sword out. His eyes bulged as I put the sword to his neck. "I swear! Please don't kill me!" I didn't.

I marched out of the dungeon and made my way up to the King's throne room. The leaders of the Humanoids (sans me) we're discussing our next move while Fafnir and James recalled the rest of the Dragon troops from Wyrmvale. I was elected to interrogate the prisoner given my title.

I could hear the yelling from outside the throne room. "I have a whole town to rebuild! You think I'm worried about rushing off to who knows where and getting more of my people killed?" the King yelled. I entered the throne room as the Dwarf leader reacted.

"A town? A TOWN? Tiamat destroyed most of Wyrmvale!! You think when he learns of his troops defeat that he won't come down and flatten your tiny little castle!" Interestingly enough it seemed like the Lionmen guards were on the side of the Dwarves.

"I agree with Tandal," I announced. The King sneered at me. "We need to take down Tiamat once and for all and end this threat for good. Even if he doesn't come himself to attack again, who says he won't send more troops down the line." Everyone in the room hollered in agreement.

"Fine," the King replied. "You and the short folk may leave and never come back. My Lionmen will stay here and rebuild. Good luck and what have you." He waved his hand dismissing us. The leader of the guard pride stood up in defiance.

"No! It is you who will stay here by yourself, coward King. Danvel and his companions fought harder than anyone else and Hourig, who I count in Danvel's pride, sacrificed himself for us all, while you sat on your throne and watched from a distance. If you were not our king I would snap your neck for such cowardice." The King nearly fell off his throne at hearing this.

"You insolent fool," he yelled. The guard leader closed the distance between him and the King in less than a second and placed his hand at his throat.

"That doesn't mean I wouldn't do it, coward King. Press me and it shall happen," he hissed. No one moved to intervene much to the King's dismay. We all started to exit the room and the Lionmen all followed. We left the castle and headed to the crater. Aturdokht had spent most of the time since Hourig... passed... here. The Dwarves had erected a monument in his likeness in record time. It was amazing what they could accomplish in only a handful of hours.

"It's time to go, Aturdokht. Fafnir is expecting us." Aturdokht barely grunted in acknowledgement. Aturdokht hadn't said a word to anyone since Hourig's passing and I wasn't going to force it. He stumbled up and followed us to the mountains. Fafnir and James had set up camp there for the returning Dragons. Most of them had already returned and we were just waiting for the last few before leaving for Axdremaria. We were gathering the forces to take down Tiamat there. I feared that it wasn't going to be enough. We needed something more.

When we reached the mountain, many of the Dwarves were saying goodbye to their loved ones and the Lionmen joined in. I met up with Murlan, Jeff, Fafnir, and James who seemed to be in deep discussion about allies. They must have had the same concern that I had.

"Even if we go against Tiamat, we will be in his element and he has an unknown amount of allies. We know there are some Water Dragons, Drakes, and Ice Dragons. Who knows what other creatures he has involved? The Ice Krakens were a surprise to us, who's to say he doesn't have something else up his sleeve," Fafnir said.

James thought on it for a little bit. "You're right. We need more allies... but who?"

"I have two options, but they might not go for it," I spoke up. They all turned to regard me and my convoy. "The Lionmen have disavowed the King and are going to battle with us and we know the Dwarves, Gnomes, and what other creatures you want to bring from Wyrmvale will help. Lynnaedra would have gathered the Water Dragons by now and the Knights of Dragonia will be with us. Then there are two races that have separated themselves from intervening already. We need to reach out to the Sand Dragons and the Behemoths. They're two forces to be reckoned with."

Everyone looked around without responding for a moment then James spoke up. "Well how do you expect to get a peaceful race to shed their ways and help us and how do we even contact the Sand Dragons?"

I smiled and pulled my pack off of Jeff's side (yes he decided he would carry it while I was interrogating the prisoner). I pulled out the whistle that the bird gave Gunther (I washed it)! I blew into it which let out a shrill tweet and within a minute several finches flew down to greet us.

"Oh, Danvel, it is you. What makes you call us at such a grave time? There is so much death happening in the world. The continent is in disarray and the water is changing. How can we simple finches be of help?" the brightest colored finch asked.

"You're right, these are grave times. But grave times are when we all need to come together and do whatever we can for victory. I need you to deliver a message, but it is a long way from here and there may be unseen dangers. The Behemoths are traversing the Dragonia/Drakeland border. Please ask them to travel to Axdremaria and meet me there. The same goes for Apollo and whatever knowledge he may be able to bring to us. The last part may be the hardest. The Sand Dragons have shut their gates to us because of Leviathan's doings. Please ask them to send an envoy to Axdremaria to discuss the state of things." The finches listened intently then chattered back and forth in their own language.

The bright one turned back to me and answered, "We shall do as you ask, Danvel. We shall also join you in Axdremaria. While we might not be fighters, we shall be your eyes ahead, scouting the unknown. Fly my friends! We shall meet you in Axdremaria!" Then the finches were gone. Hopefully this would solve the problem of allies.

After everyone's goodbyes we headed over to the docks. We were taking all of Salamandra's boats back to Dragonia and taking whatever supplies we could to help with relief there. We took the boat with James and Fafnir. I also brought Gunther along. No way was I leaving him behind again. It was a quiet boat ride back (except the barfing sounds of a seasick Jeff.)

The ride back to Axdremaria took even longer than they expected, too. Even when the waves were calm and Leviathan wasn't influencing them, it would take up to a week, but we didn't seem to be getting anywhere. The ocean and the wind were completely stagnant. We took to rowing the boat and despite fighting together it took us a long time to get into sync.

Eventually we reached Dragonian waters. "Dragons on our starboard!" Someone yelled. I rushed over to see two serpent like

Dragons riding in between us and our other ships. Then the yelling began from each ship. We were surrounded. We scrambled to arm ourselves and get the harpoons ready even though we knew it wouldn't help. Then the Dragons rose from the water and leaned over towards the boat.

"Danvel? It's me Lendra! We were patrolling the Dragonia waters for any sign of Tiamat's forces! Throw us some rope and we'll tow you the rest of the way," Lendra proposed. We all breathed a sigh of relief, and I did so doubly. I was worried that the baby Leviathan's would have turned out like their mother but they seemed to be adapting to cohabitation with humans.

We threw them some rope and attached it to our ships and off we went. We were going nearly triple the speed before (much to the dismay of Jeff). We made it in only an hour after that. Axdremaria was looking much better than when I had seen it last. People were buzzing about from this place to that, buildings were starting to rise and there was a section of tents for people who didn't have a place to stay. The most shocking discovery was that the castle had been raised. Apparently Lendra and her siblings did it as a sign of good faith and built it a new foundation.

We docked at the boats at their makeshift harbor and the group started to get on dry land. Jeff was the first one out. A group of Dragonian Knights poured out to meet us and not far behind them were Lynnaedra, Gale, and Darren. I embraced with Gale and Lynnaedra ran over to Aturdokht. He didn't say much.

"Lynnaedra, a quick word?" I asked before she asked the inevitable question. She came over and I explained what happened with Hourig to her. She teared up but swallowed it down and went to stand by Aturdokht.

"Danvel," Darren said loudly. "We are pleased to see of your return. Please bring your people to Axdremaria; I believe we all have a lot to discuss."

Chapter 15 – Best Laid Plans

Dragonia

Axdremaria

Day

The council sat quiet as I told them the tale of Salamandra. The Behemoth King, Apollo, Bernard, Darren, and Dosne, the Sand Dragon King listened intently . Sand Dragons were fierce looking creatures who consisted mostly of sand. They had wings like Drakes and were adept in manipulating the wind and the earth. The Dwarves, Gnomes, along with the two Patron Dragons sat on my side. Jeff was guarding the tent and Murlan was leading our troops with the reconstruction (not that he ever did a minute of construction in his life).

"... and that is why we need to join forces and end this threat to us all," I said, slamming my fist on the table, accidentally breaking it. The group on my side all shook their heads in agreement. The group on the other side seemed less convinced. Darren was the first to speak up.

"Danvel... we will surely fight for you, but I don't see how traversing the dangers of the north and attacking Tiamat on his own land will help us. If anything that will just leave our lands defenseless," he explained. I understood his argument but it also didn't solve things.

"That is a flawed way of viewing things, young man," Apollo countered. "Your lands are already defenseless, you just don't know it. If Tiamat rises again and visits here he will blow over the town just like he did in Heartha. He could even do it from a distance I believe," he said assuredly. This sent them back into silence.

"We will go with you," the Behemoth King announced. This was a surprise given their pacifistic nature. "The lives of the Behemoths were completely disrupted by this awful plot and too many lost their lives. We can no longer sit by and let more lives be lost. Count us all in!" This was an extreme relief. Besides the Sand Dragons, the Behemoth's represented a bulky force that could help us stand against the constant winds up north.

"If they're going then we are too," Dosne answered. "We too have sat idle for too long. The Sand Dragons are a part of this and a part of the ecosystem. We can't stay locked in our desert forever." This left the Dragonian Knights. Darren fidgeted in his chair for a moment before finally replying.

"Well then it's settled, let's go to war." He raised his fist in the air and slammed it down on the broken table like I had. It did not break with his fist   . We all cheered. Then a small voice called out from behind Apollo.

"I believe my kind is willing to help, too." Fox shot out from somewhere and appeared on the table. "The Raiju are coming, too." It was settled, we had our army.

We left the tent and I wandered over to Gale's half constructed house. The house was livable at the moment but it didn't offer much room. They had basically constructed small huts for the people to live in with the promise of building the rest of it later. The people didn't mind. It was nice to have a place that actually blocked the now frequent rains.

Gale was making dinner when I first arrived. It was nice to smell some good home cooking for a change. I snuck a bite in before I went over to get a kiss. "Did everything go well?" she asked as she embraced me.

"I suppose it depends on what you define as well," I answered. "They all agreed to come with us, but we're still going to war in an unknown territory. It's not my favorite option." I grabbed a key from the table and grabbed a blanket. "I'm headed to the castle," I said grimly. She nodded and went back to cooking.

We had put Gunther in the castle, away from everyone, for safety. We didn't want him to wake up and slaughter everyone. Only three of us had a key to the main gate. We had summoned every healer in Dragonia to try and help him, but as soon as they saw him they refused to help. The dark magic of Muramasa sent them running.

I entered the castle and lit the torches on the side. One of the benefits of it sinking was it had washed away all the blood. The people of Axdremaria had taken whatever bodies they could find and buried them. Gunther lay in the throne room (perhaps where his actual throne should be) which was the furthest from any living person. The weirdest thing is that his body seemed in a stasis. He wasn't able to eat any food and the lack of smell meant he wasn't producing any waste. It was like he was frozen in time.

I walked in and lit the torches inside (they kept snuffing out). Gunther lay on his cot, still motionless. I laid the blanket over him. "Well, buddy. Looks like I'm headed off to the north to fight Tiamat. Doesn't look like it's going to be too much fun. Snow, wind, and more snow. I don't think you'd like it very much. I know I'm not going to. If I don't come back… then you better and you better come back whole. None of the Muramasa crap."

Then I left. I tried not to stay too long. Dark magic can taint people's souls they say. I ran back to Gale's hut, the rain was starting again. Darren and Apollo were there. "I had an idea that might increase our numbers again," Darren said, acting a bit nervous.

"What is it?" I asked, stepping into the hut and sitting at our small table. Gale had a look of anger on her face so I knew I wasn't going to like whatever he had to say. I hope I didn't have to kill him.

"Well I just feel that we have an army right here that we're ignoring. Leviathan's offspring. They're numerous, strong, and I imagine they'd be willing," he proposed. I slammed my fist down onto the table in anger, breaking this one too, then stood up and got in his face.

"Are you proposing we send kids into the battle, Darren? Because that's what they are! Kids! When I found them they didn't even know what to do without their mother and at least here they found a purpose. If we send them off the battle who says they won't grow up to be just like their mother," I yelled. I pushed him out of the hut and into the now pouring rain.

"I only meant to say… it's just that they're only Dragons, sir. Basically meant to kill. Look what they did all around this continent," he tried to explain. I kicked his feet out from under him and shoved him in the mud.

"I was wrong to think you'd changed Darren. Sure you might have helped the city get back on its feet but you've only done it for the humanoids. You just perpetuated what this war is about!" People started to pour out of their huts to see what was going on. "We aren't humanoids and Dragons anymore. We're a team! Equal! Together." Darren started stuttering.

"But… but… what I mean is," he said cowering. I pulled my sword out and slammed it into the ground.

"I know what you meant, Darren. And now you're going to hear what I mean. You're done here in Axdremaria. If I ever see you again… well you won't like what I do. Now get going." I turned around, pulled my sword out, not bothering to look to see if he left. I knew he would. I entered into the hut again where Apollo was waiting patiently like he always did.

"A little harsh on him, don't you think?" Gale said in a berating voice. She had set the broken table for the three of us. We all sat down (after I dried off of course).

"We don't need people like him trying to tear down what we're building here. We have nearly every race here to create a new future. A future of real peace and unity. Hell, if I knew where the Elves were hiding out I'd reach out to them, too, and everyone hates them! We don't need people who are willing to send kids into war and counter the new start we created." She didn't argue.

"I agree with you completely," Apollo said in between bites. "Darren was just a placeholder anyways. Gale should be the new baron... well baroness." I smiled but Gale was obviously shocked by this. "She has the personality and is well-liked. I imagine that no one will have a problem with it. I'll stay here with her to help with all of the political things." Gale still said nothing.

"Well sit down and eat, honey! Nothing's decided yet! We'll announce it tomorrow and see how everyone feels about it. I'm sure they'll love it," I said with a big smile. She sat down and nibbled at her food, obviously mulling over everything in her head.

Dragonia

Axdremaria

Noon

We announced the proposal of Gale becoming the Baroness of Dragonia early in the morning and within two hours nearly everyone in Axdremaria poured out their support. They must have really loved her barmaid services. We had a short celebration and coronation and then it was back to war preparations. The Dwarves had used whatever ore we had left over in Dragonia and made new armor for those that needed it.

The Lionmen and Dragons had spent their time hunting and preparing the food and hides for the journey. The Behemoths guided the Humans on building carts for them to pull the supplies. Lastly the Gnomes harvested whatever herbs and edible plants they could from the forests and fished. We were ready to move by the time night fell. The council met in the town square for one last strategy session before heading off.

"So everyone's ready to head off?" I asked. Each selected leader shook their head yes. "I want to split us up by race, not to separate us, but to capitalize on our strengths. First," I said turning to the Behemoth King, "we need to put the Behemoth's in the center of everything. If you are going to be pulling our supplies we need to protect you." The King nodded in acknowledgement.

"Obviously we want the Sand Dragons to be watching the sky. You'd be the first to notice if a Drake would attack and if they decided to attack at our supplies there would be nothing we could do stop them without you. Maybe one Sand Dragons stationed with each of the Behemoths pulling a cart. Flying above them of course." Dosne smiled at this.

"It would be our pleasure to show those vile Drakes what it means to fly."

"Good! The Humans and the Gnomes will be on the ground protecting the supplies around the Behemoths and if we get into a battle they'll help unstrap the Behemoths from the carts so they can enter battle together. Then we move to the outer perimeter. I want the Lionmen out front," I said to Aryeh, the Lionman who threatened their King. Since then, the rest of the Lionmen swore allegiance to him.

"Your speed and ferocity will be important in catching the enemy off guard. It will give everyone else time to move into position and give the Behemoths time to enter the battle." Aryeh bared his teeth at this.

"We shall rip their throats from their bodies before they have the chance to retaliate. Then we do to them what they did to our homes!"

"Throat ripping, got it," I replied. Sounded mildly disgusting. "The Dragons will provide support on the sides," I said to Fafnir and James. They simply nodded. They knew what to do. "The Dwarves will be our rear guards since they are adept with bows and fierce in hand to hand combat," I said to Hongden, the newly elected leader of the Dwarves. "Lastly the Raiju will work with the finches to scout the perimeter. You're more attuned to magical things than we are so maybe you'll pick up something we won't." Fox didn't really react to this, but I didn't expect him to.

"Everyone clear?" I asked.

"You bet, General Danvel," James replied. Everyone cheered and went to their camps. Murlan and Jeff raced over to me after the meeting.

"Where are we going to be placed?" Murlan asked.

"Neighhhhh," Jeff said. He didn't like being forgotten.

"Well, you're with me. We have the hard job. We scout the way to the North. No one has really travelled the north extensively so we don't know which ways to go. Not even Apollo can help us with it. So we head out as soon as possible. The finches are going to let the main force know if we found a way or not. Go get our supplies and let's move," Jeff and Murlan hopped to and ran off faster than I expected.

Then Lynnaedra and Aturdokht came into view. "What about us?" Aturdokht asked. His voice had a raggedness to it that reminded me of Hourig, and it made me smile for a second. Lynnaedra wasn't looking too good. She hadn't been seen since I broke the news to her.

"I want you to stay here with the baby Leviathans. They need a family now, and I can't think of anyone better to teach them right from wrong." Aturdokht huffed at this.

"You just don't want us to get killed like my father," he replied bitterly. Even Lynnaedra was shocked at this and slapped him a little.

"You are damn right I don't want that. He died so you could live and I am not going to throw away that sacrifice. Do some good with the life that he gave you and teach these young Dragons what it means to co-exist with humans and what good we can do together. They've already done a lot of good, but they are still young and need to see what more they can do." He still didn't seem convinced.

"I'm also asking you to stay here and look after Gale and Gunther. Tiamat could have forces already on his way here so we need people who know how to fight to defend the city against them. There is nothing more important to me than this. If I could stay I would, but I'm sort of leading the charge," I said playfully hitting his shoulder.

"There are more important things than fighting, Aturdokht," Lynnaedra said. "We are building a new future here for everyone. Something that can last. Let us go meet with Lendra." They started to leave and then Aturdokht turned around.

"Thank you, Danvel. Thank you for not letting me waste what my dad sacrificed himself for," he said with a small tear forming in his eye. A tear of fire, because that's what Fire Dragons cried.

"No problem, kiddo. No problem at all." By the time they had left, Jeff and Murlan were back. Murlan was sporting some armor that had stars painted on it so it matched his regular outfit yet he still wore the miniaturized had. They had more supplies than I cared to carry, but hey, who knows what would happen in the Drakeland.

"NEIGHHH," Jeff cried and we shoved off.

Dragonia/Drakeland Border

Behemoth Camp

Night

It didn't take us long to reach the border, but when we reached the border I already knew this was going to be a tough journey. Apparently Tiamat didn't want any visitors so the winds had increased in speed dramatically the closer we got. "I already hate the north and we're not even over the border," I yelled over the winds. Murlan huffed and shoved his hat into his pack.

We kept trying to move forward but the wind would push us back. We continued to try for about fifteen minutes, but to no avail.

"Perhaps I can help," a voice yelled from behind us. It was Bernard. He moved in front of us and blocked the wind. We pushed forward and eventually we got past the winds that we're blocking the border. Beyond that it seemed to be just a normal wintery day.

"Bernard! What brings you up here with us?" I asked, slightly out of breath. That wind can really take it out of you.

"The little King ordered it," he replied. "Thought that it might be good to have my bulk to help along the way. And look, it already has." He shook off some of the snow he had collected from the wind and we started to walk.

"Well it's good to have to you along," I replied.

"Neighhh," Jeff added. We started our trek forward into the north. I was hoping Bernard had some sense of direction because I really didn't have any idea where we were heading. We travelled on for a few hours before we had our first encounter with a finch and a Raiju.

"What's the report," I said as we all took a break and ate some to regain some energy.

"Just keep going straight and you'll reach a ghost town. It can serve as a base for now, I think," the finch reported.

"Still no sign of the Yeti's," the wolf Raiju said. "We are expanding our search eastward." He was a lot more rugged than Fox's wolf form was. He wore what appeared to be scars over various parts of his body, although I don't know what kind of wound would give a magical creature scars.

"Accompany us to the ghost town," I said to the both of them. I had a sneaking suspicion that something we couldn't detect was going on. We all moved forward and in about an hour we reached the town. It was mostly destroyed on the outskirts of town. Obviously there had been a battle. The Raiju and Murlan both recoiled as we entered the town.

"What is it?" I asked as I pulled my sword. They both fell over and almost passed out. As quickly as the spell started it was over. We rushed over to them and helped them up.

"An extremely dark magic was present here," Murlan explained. "Not as strong as Muramasa but more potent. Like it's magic seeped more than Muramasa's. It infected the ground here and that's why no snow lies here." He was right. In a circle around the town the ground was bare but there had to be half a foot of snow outside of it.

"Stay alert. Check the houses for supplies and with any luck a damned map," I ordered as I entered a nearby house. Everywhere I looked things were gray as if the dark magic had sapped the color from everything. There were many supplies, most of them spoiled. I looked to see if they had any books but there was nothing except cookbooks.

I popped out of the house and moved onto the next one. More of the same. It wasn't until the fifth house that I found something useful. There was a book titled 'Secrets of the North.' As I skimmed through it I got the sense that there was much hidden in the snows of Drakeland. Some of it seemed to mirror accounts from Asgard. Tales of Frost Giants and a terrible serpent. Eventually it got to the location of Hyperborea.

"Crap," I said as I read on. "This won't be easy. Not one bit." The book depicted the magical properties of the city. That the city was not able to be accessed unless 'one accepted the reign of the snow.' I ran out into the town and got the finch's attention. "Tell the council to meet me here; we have some things to discuss." The finch flew off and we set up camp.

Chapter 16 - The Abominable Snow City

Drakeland

Ghost Town

Sunrise

The council arrived as we were waking up. We had found a few more books that helped us paint a better picture of how to travel the north but none that had helped us solve the mystery of the phrase. When they entered, all the magical creatures had the same spell wash over them that Murlan and the Raiju did.

We met at what had to have been the town square and discussed the phrase. "I never really thought it would have been a magical city that he was in. Maybe magical creatures can enter and physical can't," Fafnir mused. He might be right. Yetis were the least magical of the humanoids, coming in at around one percent.

"Then we'll keep a Raiju with us so that if they see the city, we'll know for sure. Make sure you all keep your Raiju close and up front as well." We showed them around what we found in the town and suggested they use it as a landmark and start making some maps with the finches help and then my group was off.

It was nice being able to move in a small group instead of having to worry about the needs of so many at the moment, but I knew it would be short lived. We tried to take the paths that the book told us about it, but we were wary of what looked like recent changes to them. Trees were blocking the path and a new path was made, yet there were no trees nearby. Snow drifts would have seemed to cover the path, but there was no sign of recent snowstorms.

We spent a lot of time digging through snow to find the old paths. We ended up making a sort of plow out of a tree and hooking it to the front of Jeff who loved the idea that he could just push the snow out of the way with ease. With the plow on Jeff's neck, it didn't take us long till we reached the point 'where all snowstorms meet.' We could tell it was here because the snow's height was dramatically higher. I couldn't see anything. Only Bernard could see above it, and his eyes were useless in detecting magic.

We all climbed up him and peered over the snow piles. Murlan and the Raiju nearly fell over, but this time out of shock. "What do you see?" I asked. Surprisingly, the Raiju was the one without the words to speak.

"It's magnificent and terrible. The structures are absolutely beautifully crafted and big enough to hold all our forces, but also their forces. And their forces are immense. Bigger than I think we expected. There are also three other buildings, one corresponding with each snow pile. I didn't get to see anything of importance in them but if I were to guess, they were prisons," Murlan said grimly.

I turned to the Raiju and shook him a little to snap him out of it. "Don't worry about their numbers. We have the element of surprise and hopefully the advantage of teamwork. You're the fastest here, so tell me if you can get in there." The Raiju quickly regained its composure. He shook his head and dashed in between the four snow piles. He decided to take a right towards what seems to be the lesser guarded prison and as soon as he walked past the snow pile I couldn't see him anymore.

"What do you see, Murlan?" I asked, nudging him. He looked hard at where the Raiju went in and smiled.

"He's in. He changed into his cat form and is sneaking around. Wait a minute... he rounded the corner and I lost him." We waited anxiously for a few minutes before he returned. He jumped up on top of Bernard and surprised us all. I guess his cat form was much harder to see than we expected.

"That's where they're keeping the Yetis. Probably a thousand or so of them. It won't be hard to break them out, though. There are only two guards," he reported.

"If that's where they are keeping the Yeti, and it's the least guarded, what are they keeping in the two other prisons?" Murlan thought out loud. He had a good point. Yetis were great warriors and in history were known to have won great battles against Dragons.

The Raiju went back to the four snow pillar and this time chose the one of the left. Murlan kept following him and until he rounded a corner again.

This time we waited substantially longer until he jumped back up. "This one isn't a prison per se. They have several wizards in there. I assume they are the ones casting the spells. They could get up and walk out but I believe somehow they are all conjoined by the spell. They all would shift in the same direction anytime an Ice Dragon got near and everything they did was in unison."

Murlan stood up and looked into the prison again. His eyes focused in a way I had never seen before. "He's right. There's a whole lot of magic coming out from the portal they have. It's spreading out all across Drakeland." He unfocused his eyes and then looked back at us.

"So you can see magic? Never heard of a wizard being able to do that," I said.

"Well it's not common knowledge and it takes years of training you know. I did actually happen to be a pretty good wizard when I wasn't making a mistake," he said with a smile. The Raiju turned back around and went to the last prison which was right where we were. According to Murlan it was the most heavily guarded.

This time I didn't expect that the Raiju was coming back. There was no commotion, but he was gone for nearly twenty minutes. We were about ready to send a finch to get reinforcements when he popped back out. "Perhaps this is the most interesting find. A massive Dragon. Bigger than your descriptions of Tiamat. He has white skin and claims that you know him. Says his name was Galen." Jeff and I reeled at this.

"Galen was a merchant in Axdremaria, not a Dragon. I mean sure he was a little strange, but to be the size you mention, he'd have to be very old," I said stunned.

"Perhaps he fell under the same problem as us all, Danvel," Bernard spoke up. "Leviathan and Tiamat wanted us out of the way, so maybe they wanted him out of the way, too. What better way to get an old and powerful Dragon out of the way than to make him human?" His words sounded right. Especially after the way Galen acted the last time I saw him.

"And when I killed Leviathan that broke the curse. That was when Galen mysteriously disappeared. I thought I was just going a bit crazy," I said laughing a bit.

"Neighhh," Jeff echoed. Then he sniffed the air and hunched down. "Neigh neigh neighhh neigh neighh whinny neighhhh," he said. Someone was nearing us from behind. A scent that wasn't one of our troops. Everyone remained still as I slid down Bernard and stalked my way over to them. I could see the body through the snow so I launched myself at them and placed my blade at their neck. It was Darren.

"What the hell are you doing here?" I whispered close to him. "We're in enemy territory. You're going to get us all killed." I pulled the blade off his neck and put it in my sheath.

"I wanted to prove to you that I wasn't some coward who was against you. I came to help! I travelled the north trying to find you and I just got your tracks maybe an hour ago," he explained desperately.

"Fine, just stay close and don't speak loudly. We are literally in the enemy's camp," I said emphasizing the loudly part. We didn't need some halfwit pushing us into battle too soon.

We crawled back up to Bernard where Jeff was just sending off a finch. All that was left to do was figure out how to send a physical being through the portal.

Drakeland

Hyperborea

Nightfall

Each of the physical creatures had taken a turn at trying to figure out what 'accept the reign of the snow' actually meant. I had just sat there and hoped that by not doing anything that would be acceptance, but nothing changed. Jeff tried to use his makeshift plow to move some of it and reveal some kind of symbol but that didn't work. Bernard tried rolling around in the snow, which didn't work but was highly amusing to watch.

I had gone back to sitting in the middle of the portals when a snowstorm began to pour in from the east. As the snow began to pour over me I could suddenly see into the portal where the Yetis were being held. I jumped up and ran back to the group. "I figured it out! I forgot that the Yetis are morons! It isn't 'accept the reign of the snow'. 'It's accept the rain of the snow!' like the snow pouring down on us."

We sent another finch off to let the main group that we were initiating the attack plan. They were waiting just on the edge of the city and we were going to release the Yeti's, the Dragon, and the wizards... not in that particular order. When the city showed up in the physical world again, we were going to attack. We all went towards the portal and launched ourselves into the Yeti prison (except for Bernard who I was afraid would make too much of a ruckus in such a small space).

I pulled out Fail-not and shot two arrows blindly. Sure enough they ricocheted off the walls and stuck the only two guards in the heart. We searched their bodies for keys and found them. The Yeti were locked up in some communal prison and looked as if they had been there for a long time. Their fur was mottled with blood and dirt and other stains that I didn't really want to think about.

"Listen, I'm going to let you all out, but you have to be quiet and listen to exactly what I say," I explained to the one wearing a crown. I was really hoping he was their leader and not just some crazy person wearing a crown.

"Hokdachow. Carenboran snoglefich," he replied proudly. I didn't know what the hell it meant, I was just hoping he understood what I said. I unlocked the door and we all walked out slowly and without sound. When we got them out I pointed to Bernard.

"Follow that huge hunk of beast and he'll get you out of the area safely," I said trying to convey what I meant.

Bernard helped by saying, "Donkeldingo Bernard. Flargendorsle bankenlots hagerbater globle." I hate other languages. The Yeti King seemed to respond to this and turned to his race.

"Ashtarinen! Fangen globle," he yelled and they all ran off chasing after Bernard. The good thing was that we saved the all the Yeti. The bad thing was that was by far the easiest part. I stationed Darren inside the east prison in case they had a secret entrance we didn't know about. The rest of us sat and waited for the next snowstorm to start.

I decided it was a good enough time to risk it and we made a small camp outside and ate. Bernard was back before the storm started. "The Yeti returned to their homes and after they take care of

their injured and what have you, they promised to return to aid us."
After he came back, it was still two more hours until the next
snowstorm started. It was coming from the west.

"Well I guess we're knocking down the portals before we
save that Dragon. You ready for this Murlan?" I asked helping him
from the ground. He was going to try and take the entirety of the
spell on himself to release the wizards from their prison. Then he
would cancel the spell. It was more complicated than it sounded.

Bernard waited on the outside again, this time to guide the
wizards back to safety. We charged in again and followed basically
the same plan. I shot out a bunch of arrows, killing most of the
Drakes. The rest were silenced by Jeff who was in rare form. There
were about twenty wizards in a square around some kind of crystal.
The crystal was glowing in a pulsing rainbow.

Murlan walked over to the nearest one and grabbed ahold of
her. His eyes immediately started to mirror theirs. His body took on
their rigidity and essentially he became one of them. Then he moved
his foot to the left. None of them followed but they all turned to look
at them. He continued to do this until some of them started to follow.

As they started to follow him, he drew in their power and released

them from the square.

When they were released they all fell over stunned.

Eventually it came down to Murlan and some old fart who was

trying to stay in control. Murlan's aura started to glow and then the

man was released from the spell. He kept hold of the spell as we

rushed over to help the wizards. This ended up being a mistake. The

first wizard shot a bolt of lightning out towards us. The Raiju

jumped in front of it and easily absorbed it.

"You fools! You'll never stop the dark magic that is

coming," another one yelled. It was all out war between us and about

twenty wizards. The Raiju did his best to block the incoming shots

while I dispatched of them, but he couldn't be everywhere at once.

Jeff and I took a few hits and retreated.

"Neighhhh," Jeff said angrily.

"I know! What ungrateful bastards." I pulled out the bow and

unleashed whatever arrows I had left. When we dove back around

the corner the Raiju was facing off against last wizard, the one who

had given Murlan so much trouble. The Raiju did a full force

lightning jump at him, but it seemed he was ready for it and trapped the Raiju in some magic bubble. It kept getting smaller and then the Raiju was gone. The wizard was laughing when I cut off his head.

The crystal that the wizards were standing around when we found began pulsing more frequently and Murlan's aura began to glow more brightly. I grabbed my sword and struck the crystal as hard as I could. It started to crack, but Murlan didn't react. I struck it again and this time it shattered. Murlan broke free of the spell and all hell broke loose. Almost immediately the two forces began meeting in battle. We ran out of the prison before it crashed down on top of us. Darren met us in the middle as his prison shelter was destroyed, too.

Above us the Sand Dragons were unleashing a fury against the Drakes. They would break apart into sand particles and use that to bring the Drakes down. Once on the ground the ground forces swarmed them. That was about the only place we were doing well. The Ice Dragons had the advantage of strategic placing and the Water Dragons that we're on their side were combining their powers with Ice Dragons to make them more potent.

The Behemoths were having trouble getting into the battle because of the building left little room for them to move. Some had taken to smashing the buildings over to make room for the others. Bernard joined in with them and began tearing down the prison debris that was in the way. The Behemoths poured in and began blocking the Dragon's attacks so that more of our forces could move in.

James and Fafnir moved in to meet us. "Tiamat must be in the main building," I yelled to them. Fafnir dashed off towards it and left James and us to fend off the closing forces. Ice Dragons had begun forming ice slides over the Behemoths to meet the smaller ground forces. James, Jeff, and I took the fight to the arriving Ice Dragons while Murlan shrunk their ice slides. This was causing them to topple over and left them at the mercy of the Lionmen.

We showed no quarter to those in front of us and forgot the ones behind us (including the Dragon in the third prison). We climbed up the stairs that led to the main chamber. Water Dragons blocked path so James tore a piece off the side of the building and smashed it on top of them. Jeff and I jumped on top of it to make sure they were dead (we knew they were dead but it was a lot of fun).

We fought the rest of the way up, cutting a swath through the enemy lines while the rest of our forces kept fighting. We reached the chamber only to witness a terrible sight. Tiamat had Fafnir pinned to the ground and defenseless. Before we had a chance to stop him, Tiamat bit down on Fafnir's neck, killing him instantly. Tiamat picked up Fafnir's lifeless body and threw it over at us.

"Come to meet your deaths, have you?" Tiamat said with a sneer. He flapped his wings, sending us all flying. We ran back up the stairs to meet the oncoming winds. He kept flapping making us hold onto the railing for support.

"How are we going to get close to him?" I yelled over the roaring winds.

"How the hell am I supposed to know?" James yelled back. "I can barely move myself!"

"Neigh neighhh," Jeff called.

"That's a damned great and awful idea," I yelled back. I pulled out my sword and held it tight to me.

"What did that crazy horse of yours say?" James replied.

"SLEIPNIR! And he said that you should throw me. You're pretty great at throwing rocks and I'm a hell of a lot lighter than them!" He smiled and shook his head yes. He grabbed me and threw me with all of his force. I could feel the wind blowing hard against my face as I flew through the air. Tiamat began to beat his wings harder in hopes of stopping me but it wasn't working. I slammed into him sword first, cutting off his right wing.

I tucked and rolled coming out facing Tiamat's back and my sword at the ready. He screamed in agony and burst out of the building before falling into the snow. We rushed out of the building after him. He kept trying to take flight and then would smash into the ground. When we made it out of the city, he turned around to take us in and then howled as loud as he could.

James threw a large piece of dirt at him, hitting him square on the head and shutting him up. Jeff ran over and tackled him, knocking him over, but sending Jeff flying away. The battle started to spill over towards us as the enemy tried to protect Tiamat. I began to charge at Tiamat when an Ice Dragon blindsided me. My sword and helmet went flying and I slammed hard into the ground. The Ice Dragon worked its way over and formed an ice spear. I tried to back away but I couldn't gain any footing. Apparently it had frozen the ground underneath me. Right as he was about to drive it down into me, Darren came smashing into it, intercepting the spear in his left arm. He knocked it over and rolled over on the ground, grabbing my sword. He lifted it, no small feat for any man let alone one with only one usable arm, and slammed it down into the Ice Dragon.

I got up after a few tries and ran over to Darren. "See, I'm not… all that bad," he said, exhausted. I picked him up off the ground and grabbed my sword. I snapped the ice spear near the entrance to his wound and helped him away from the battle.

"Stupid stuff like that is how you're going to get yourself killed, Darren," I said, setting him down.

"Better me than you," he said dryly. "You can end this war, Danvel. Do it." He pushed me away and I ran back into the battle. James and Jeff were giving it to Tiamat pretty good, but his massive size had them overmatched. For every blow they landed, he landed one back. I ran through the battle, cutting down whoever got in my way.

When I finally reached them, Jeff was unconscious with Tiamat standing on top of him, ready to put him out of his misery. James was circling trying to find a way to stop him from killing Jeff. "See, it is as I said," Tiamat said in a labored voice. "You shall only find your death here." Then a white blur came by, knocking Tiamat off of Jeff and into the ground. He stood up over Tiamat for a minute and then ended his life.

He roared and all of Tiamat's forces seemed to back down. We drew closer ready to attack when he tucked his wings and laughed. "You have nothing to fear with me, Danvel and company. I am Bahamut, the Patron of light. You once knew me as the human, Galen. I was cursed by Nidhogg, that filthy creature, to become human and service his purpose in any way I could. It was how Muramasa was unleashed and how the Golem's were struck by the petrification curse."

I ran over to Jeff and helped him up. He was starting to regain consciousness again. "Bahamut? Nidhogg? We've never heard of these Dragons before." Even James seemed puzzled.

"That is because we were supposed to intervene if something like this had ever happened. We were supposed to stop the Dragons from fighting with the Humanoids and vise verse, but before I could intervene, I found that Nidhogg, the Patron of the Dark, had planned all of this and he cursed me to stop me from interfering."

"But I never did count on the blasted Dragon Slayer being such a nuisance," a voice called from an unknown place. The ground began to shake violently, knocking everyone over and causing the city to crumble. A massive hole formed where the city was, swallowing and anyone that was in it. Nidhogg emerged. He had a larger serpent body like Leviathans but it was twice as thick. He boasted the same dark aura that creatures imbued by dark magic seemed to have.

The rest of the armies scattered out of the way (Bernard had picked up Darren and Jeff and sprinted away) leaving me, James and Bahamut to take care of Nidhogg. Nidhogg turned, regarding us and then spat dark breath out at us. I saw James dig a hole into the ground before it hit him and Bahamut swung by and grabbed me.

"I know this is the wrong time, but why didn't you tell me you were cursed?" I said as he carried me above Nidhogg. We flew fast! Bahamut shot a salvo at Nidhogg, hitting him along his body and causing him to reposition himself.

"It was part of the curse! I couldn't reveal anything about their plan or hinder it directly. That's why I assisted you in the most indirect ways as possible. Are you ready?"

I gave him the thumbs up and he let out another salvo at Nidhogg, but this time he dropped me at the same time. I pulled out my sword and as I descended I stuck it in his side, causing a huge gash. I lost my momentum about three hundred feet from the ground so I pulled myself up and jumped on to his back.

Bahamut kept unleashing salvos on him as I pulled out my sword. His blood was even more toxic than the Chaos Dragons and I almost fell off, but caught myself at the last moment. James had launched himself out of the ground, similarly to Nidhogg, and was atop him like I was. He apparently didn't like us where being on top of him so he slammed his body onto the ground, knocking us both off.

James grabbed me and pulled me underground with him just as Nidhogg was about to roll over us. I shoved my sword up and he rolled over it, creating another deep gash. We popped out of the hole after he was gone to see Bahamut descend upon him with extreme speed. Whatever Nidhogg had in mass and power, he was being made a fool of by Bahamut's speed and prowess. Every shot he made hit a wound we had made on Nidhogg and dug chunks into him.

"You fools. You won't win. Soon I'll kill everything and have the planet to myself," Nidhogg said as he slammed hard down on the ground. We both fell over. Nidhogg towered over us and unleashed his dark breath on us. Just as it was about to hit us, Bahamut flew in and took the blast for us, sending him flying into the ground injured. As Nidhogg raged at us, both forces began to sneak their way out on to the battlefield. James and I did our best to keep his attention away from Bahamut, but we were losing steam ourselves. Nidhogg unleashed another blast at us and James pulled us underground at the last second.

"We can't keep this up, Danvel. Without Bahamut in the fight, he's just too big," James said out of breath. I tried to reply but I was out of breath, too.

"He can't win," I finally spat out.

"Stop! What are you doing?" we heard from above. We jumped out of the hole to see the forces, Tiamat's and ours, surrounding Nidhogg. Bahamut was on his feet again and then they all attacked. Nidhogg was overwhelmed as everyone unleashed their anger upon him. Bahamut flew by and picked me up.

"We need a finishing blow, Danvel. Nidhogg is reeling from this attack, but he can recover from it. Take it to him." He dropped me going at extreme speeds and I basically flew towards Nidhogg. With my sword extended I slammed right into him, striking him in between the eyes. He writhed in agony but didn't fall down so I pulled out the sword and struck at him again. Three strikes later he fell over, dead.

He crashed to the ground, flinging me far away. I lay down for a while, feeling the aches wash across my body. Eventually, I stood up and made my way back to the battlefield. Tiamat's forces stood at the opposite of ours, the tension building between them. James and Bahamut were trying to calm them all down to no avail. I ran, or hobbled, my way to the center, sticking my sword into the ground. The bickering forces became silent.

"It stops here," I said meagerly. "No more fighting." An Ice and Water Dragon, followed by Wind Drake moved in front of their forces. They were impressive in size and obviously the oldest of the bunch. They had scars covering a large portion of their body and the one was missing its eye.

"We are the leaders of our tribes," the Wind Drake spoke. "I am Bora, and this is Glacia and Kawthar," he said pointing to the Ice Dragon and Water Dragon respectively. "We surrender and wish for peace." They all knelt. Behind me the yelling started again. I raised my hand and they all grew silent again.

I sat down in the snow and leaned against my sword. "I wish for peace too, you know. But you know we need assurances. What changed your mind?" Bora stood up and then stepped forward.

"We were... misled. Tiamat promised us our own lands without having to coexist with the Humanoids. We were not aware of Nidhogg at all. There is no forgiveness for what we have done and some of us may not even seek forgiveness, but we no longer want war and we no longer want death. We will take whatever answer you give us as punishment."

I stood up slowly and turned towards our people. The leaders of each faction, at least those that were left, stepped forward. Aryeh, James, Dosne, Fox, Bahamut, and Bernard stepped forward. Jeff came forward with a battered Hongden on his back and Murlan aided Darren to the front. "What do you all have to say?" They started in order.

"We should kill them now. Be done with their vile trespasses and let us all rest at ease," Aryeh spat.

"I don't really know. Nidhogg, Tiamat, and Leviathan were behind all of this. Can we really fault them all?" James countered.

"How can you create a peace for everyone with such distrust? We can't go back to the way things were," Dosne said.

"It is a curious thing, to wage a war and then expect peace. I don't think even my people would be comfortable with it," Fox said with surprising emotion.

"Find the balance, Danvel," Bahamut counseled.

"I say curse them to be nomads. Never to have a land of their own," Bernard said in a cruel tone. I imagined he was incredibly bitter at the death of the Behemoth King in battle which now thrusted Benedict into leadership too soon.

Hongden reached and placed his hand on my shoulder. "Peace… Danvel. Peace." Jeff took him back to his people.

Lastly, Murlan led Darren over to me. He looked awful. Despite the fact that I broke the ice spear in half, it must have continued to spread throughout him. "Danvel… I know I don't have long, but I think it's time for my speech for you," he said coughing up a little blood. "You're trying too hard to save everyone when you can't. You tried to save me, but I was always a coward and narrow-minded. There is no one fix all solution. You didn't save me and you won't save all of them." And then he died.

It was a strange feeling. I had experienced the death of close friends and the near-death of someone I viewed like a son. Saw comrades slaughtered and relived the death of my parents. But it didn't all hit me until then. I began to cry for all of the deaths around me and caused by me. No one said anything. After a few moments, I rose, wiping the tears from my eyes.

"You'll have your land to yourselves. We will split the north in two," I said loudly. There were many grumblings within both camps. "You will take the north eastern part where there are no human cities. No Humanoids will be allowed on your land except members of this council, as you are now becoming part of it. You must build your own cities, however, since we have to rebuild countless of our own because of you. You also cannot freely roam in our lands. You are condemned to stay on your land unless you are an approved dual citizen. Approval by the council, only. Anyone else will be tried by the council to suffer any punishment we deem necessary. Does anyone object to this?"

I bet that there were probably many objections, but we all were tired of fighting. "Then it's settled," a voice from behind us said. We all turned to find Apollo standing in a massive archway which led to Axdremaria. "Please all wounded come through first." Our army started filing into the archway and out of sight. Bora came up to me and held out his hand...claws... mitts.

"Thank you, Danvel. You surely are a great warrior in more ways than one. We shall begin by making our home here in Hyperborea. We will be in contact if anything happens," he said shaking my hand.

"Wait just a minute there," Apollo called coming over. "If all the members of the council would stay here, please. We are not finished." Bora turned to his people and ordered them to begin cleanup of what was left of Hyperborea. "You're looking a little worse for wear, Danvel."

"Neighh," Jeff said tackling me.

"I'm glad we're okay too, buddy. Maybe after this we can have some quality Jeff and Dan time," I replied as I ran my hand through his mane. Finally, the rest of our forces filed through the archway. Apollo closed the doors and then knocked on them three times. When he opened up, a room I hadn't seen before appeared.

"All members of the council please come through," Apollo ordered. We all listened.

Chapter 17 - The End?

I really don't know

We all sat down in the chairs that lined the glamorous room we were in. It wasn't one of the rooms that Apollo normally used. It was a deep red that was almost mesmerizing. There were golden lamps all throughout, casting an uneasy light on all of us. Apollo moved in front of us and raised his hands.

"I know you're probably wondering why I asked you all here. You all had what I would call a busy day, but there are missing parts of the story that some of you don't know. Parts that are necessary to see what will happen next." He lowered his hands and let out a slow exhale.

"The history of this continent is steeped in war between Humanoid and Dragons, Dragons and Dragons, and sometimes Humanoid and Humanoid. Eventually, there was a balance made. The Dragons were split up by territory as were the humans. The Dragon King and Dragon Council were made to govern affairs between the Dragon and Humanoids. This worked for a long time, but eventually another war broke out and the Humanoids and Dragons were at war again. The Dragon King was killed and the Dragon Council disbanded." Everyone shook their head knowing the history.

"That was when the Dragon Slayers were created. Originally fifty were made to end the war, and they did. Many died in this war, but eventually a long peace started between the two races. Or at least we thought. It was at that time Nidhogg started to move things into place. Nidhogg and Bahamut are the oldest of the Patron Dragons and were originally the only two. Patrons of Dark and Light respectively. Most people know their titles but didn't know the implication. They were responsible for the light and dark on the continent. Bahamut's magic helped the day come to pass and Nidhogg brought the night sky."

"After the Dragon Slayers won the war, it was decided that the Dragon magic had to be more spread out and not governed by just two Dragons. The Water, Earth, Wind, and Fire Patrons were created. Then the countries we know today began to form. Nidhogg and Bahamut were to choose two patrons each. Bahamut chose Fafnir and Adhamhnan while Nidhogg chose Tiamat and Leviathan. Thus he had his two pawns."

"Nidhogg made his next move. Knowing that Bahamut would see whatever he did from his sky temple, Nidhogg got Leviathan to procure a powerful curse from Morgan le Fay. It would turn Bahamut into a human and curse him to help whatever way he could with Nidhogg's plan."

"Since Bahamut saw much from his sky temple, he knew the location of evil things. Things that shouldn't have been raised. Muramasa. The Petrifying Orb. Countless others. Bahamut did not sit idle, however. He procured a shop and uncovered great mythological items which might help aid in ridding him of the curse."

"While Bahamut did all of these things, tragic events happened. Danvel's parents were killed leaving him heir to all the Dragon Slayer magic, and Gunther, the heir to the Dragon King line, lost his parents as well. I took Danvel under my wing, as such was the custom and steered him best as I could. Nidhogg had won his war. He had moved everything into place. Tiamat would wipe out the Wyrmvale while Leviathan would take care of Dragonia. Then together those two would finish Salamandra. What Leviathan and Tiamat didn't know was what their actions were causing."

"With the chaos that Leviathan and Tiamat were to bring, Nidhogg would finally be free from his cage. The cage that he was put in by the Asgardians so he would not bring about Ragnarok, the end of all. However, he did not succeed."

I stood up and slammed my foot in anger, everyone was shocked. "You and I both know that you have knowledge that you couldn't possibly have Apollo and now that I know that you know all of this. How is it that you didn't warn us? The amount of lives lost! The people dear to us!" This caused an uproar with the rest of the council. Apollo raised his arms again and we eventually grew silent.

"Once, you told a young man we all have our burdens to bear, Danvel. I know the future, yes. It is a blessing and a curse. It is the curse that prevented me from telling you. I can know all the future, in fact I know most of them. It's why I am blind. But I cannot directly interfere. It is my burden. But let's say I told a particularly chatty bird with a love for gossip that Murlan had been cursed by the Dwarven Queen. Then that bird spread that around until eventually it was whispered into Murlan's ear. Well he would be forced to run back to Wyrmvale and try to get his curse reversed."

"Let's say I didn't do this, then Murlan never goes to Wyrmvale, you never come to see me to find him and you aren't in Wyrmvale when Tiamat's forces attack, Danvel. You get killed after a long night of drinking by assassins of Leviathan and Nidhogg gets his wish and brings about Ragnarok."

"Instead you come to me seeking the location of Murlan. Along the way you save the Behemoths from a terrible fate. When you get to Wyrmvale you save nearly the whole population from utter destruction. You head back to Axdremaria and nearly save everyone there. And so on," Apollo went on. "I do what I can." The council all seemed to relax when they heard this although I imagine some of them were uneasy to know that someone could change so much with just a bit of a gossip.

"I tell you all of this so you understand this truth:, the war may be over but our peril is not," Apollo continued. "Four of our six Patron Dragons have been killed which will send our ecosystem into decay. The seas have already grown still and soon the rivers will stop flowing and the rain will either become overwhelming in some places or simply cease in others. The wind will stop blowing leaving boats stranded at sea. Seeds won't spread and the land will get barren. Fires will produce little heat and warmth will seep out of all of us. Night will stop coming. We need to find someone to fill these spots."

Bahamut rocketed out of his chair as Apollo finished. Perhaps a bit too soon as he fell to one knee in pain. He quickly recovered. "We need something new. We've seen that one species cannot be given this much power. We need new totems. James and I will retain our status, but we need new species in the other roles."

Bahamut turned to the council. "How do we vote on this matter?" It was a unanimous yes.

"The Council of Draco has been formed and made its first vote," Apollo heralded. "Any volunteers on finding replacements?" James rose almost immediately, surprising everyone.

"I will go. I think I know what we're going to need to look for… plus, I have experience," he said with a wry smile. The council accepted his involvement and then waited for other replies. I turned to Jeff and gave him a pat on his side.

"What do you think, buddy? One more adventure? I mean, who doesn't like saving a continent twice in a row," I said with a smile.

Jeff dove off his seat and in front of everyone," NEIGH! Neighhhhh neighhh," he belted out. I stood up and joined him and James. No one else volunteered. They had a continent to rebuild. After a few bits of chatter between everyone, Apollo stood up and walked to a hallway connected to the room. I didn't remember seeing it when we came into the room. There were at least twenty-five doors in it.

"These doors are your route home, esteemed members of the Council of Draco. Choose any door and it will take you to where you desire." Nearly everyone eagerly filed out to return home. This left Bahamut, Jeff, James, Murlan, Apollo, and myself in the room.

"I have a surprise for you, young adventurers," Bahamut said with a smile. "While it is a great tragedy that we lost our fellow Patron Dragons, we have been imbued with an overabundance of Dragon Magic. I can help you all out. Murlan, if you wish your curse is gone. And the same can be done with you, Jeff and Danvel."

Murlan excitedly threw his hat in the air and jumped up and down. "Fix me, fix me please," he called. Bahamut laid his hand on Murlan's head and Murlan began to glow. After a few moments, Bahamut released him and Murlan looked... exactly the same. He pulled out a small wand and waved it over at one of the chairs. It exploded in a burst of fireworks. Apollo stamped his foot in anger, but Murlan didn't seem to care. "I'M CUREEEEDD," he yelled at the top of his lungs.

When he settled down I walked with him over to the hallway. "So you're not going to come with us on this one?" I asked patting him on the back.

"I think it's time to get back to my magic and remember how to do most of this stuff. It's been a true adventure and you know what I learned? I really hate adventures. I just want to get back to doing what I do," he explained. He took his hat off and gave me a hug. I did not appreciate it.

"You've taught me too much, Danvel. Too much about what I hate in myself. I'll see you some other time." Then he was gone.

I went back to where Bahamut was waiting with Jeff and James. "So how about it, Danvel? Ready to return to normal size?" He started to lay his hands on Jeff and me but Jeff stopped him.

"Neigh! Neigh," he yelled. I looked at him and patted his side.

"Are you sure?" He shook his head yes. "Can you help Gunther instead?" Bahamut closed his eyes in concentration and after a few seconds, opened them again.

"You understand, that means you both will be stuck like this? Forever. Without the crystal the Dwarf Queen had, no one else could fix you," Bahamut stated.

I shook my head yes. "I think my future wife would appreciate us being the same size," I said with a chuckle. "By the way… That guy in Wyrmvale that I gave that stone to. He looked exactly like you and behaved in the exact same way. What's that all about?"

Bahamut responded with a great laughter. "When they cursed me they wanted a body that wouldn't raise any suspicions or make anyone think I was anything special. So they modeled me after him. I was thrilled," he said with abundant sarcasm. He led us over to Apollo was patiently waiting. We said our goodbyes to him and went to the hallway. We opened a door and all exited.

Axdremaria

The Castle Formerly Known as Leviathan Castle

Night

We all fell through the door and James landed on top of us, smooshing Jeff and me. It was not a pleasant experience. Bahamut pushed him off and walked over to Gunther. He laid his hand on him and Gunther began to glow. Gunther woke up suddenly and shot up out of the bed. "What the hell?" he yelled. "Who, what, when, where! What's going on?"

"You're going to be okay, is what," I replied. Gunther rushed over to see us, tripping over his cot, getting back up then tripping on his own feet. I helped him up and gave him a hug. "It's good to see you upright." Jeff joined in on the hug. After the hug, Bahamut pulled James and me aside.

"I didn't heal him all the way, Danvel. He is bonded to Muramasa. It cannot leave his side. I built a wall around the darkness but I don't even know if that will last a single day. Even that used most of my magic. You have to watch him closely. Both of you." It wasn't great news, but heck, I was still glad to get Gunther back. "I do believe I have a sky temple to reclaim now. I'll be seeing you all soon." Bahamut flew off leaving us to figure out what to do next.

We all piled out of the castle and headed to Gale's hut to tell the Baroness the good news. I ran ahead of everyone and opened the door. Gale was asleep so I gently shook her. She woke up and began batting at me immediately. "Quit it," I yelled. She blinked her eyes a bit and then tackled me with a hug.

"You're okay!" She smothered me with kisses. "I'm so glad you're okay! And you're back so soon." I filled her in on what happened and how Nidhogg was behind it all. Just as I was about to tell her I needed to go on another adventure, she interrupted me.

"Before you go any farther, I have news of my own. News for us both! I'm pregnant!"

The End

Made in the USA
Charleston, SC
28 January 2016